The Incredible Adventures of Absolutely Normal

A Novel By

Amanda Rotach Lamkin

This book is a work of fiction. Names, characters, places, and incidents are a product of the author's imagination or are used fictitiously. Any resemblance to any persons or locales, living or deal, is entirely coincidental.

THE INCREDIBLE ADVENTURES OF ABSOLUTELY NORMAL
Copyright ©2021 Line By Lion Publications
www.pixelandpen.studio
ISBN 978-1-948807-43-2

Cover Design by Thomas Lamkin Jr. www.tljonline.com
Editing by Vikki Becker of Enchanted Editing

All rights reserved. In accordance with the U.S. Copyright Act of 1976, the scanning, uploading, and electronic sharing of any part of this book without the permission of the author is unlawful piracy and the theft of the author's intellectual property. If you would like to use material from the book (other than for review purposes), prior written permission must be obtained by contacting the publisher. Thank you for respecting author rights.

To all of those still waiting for a letter delivered by owl, a magical wardrobe, or an unexpected party. The adventure is in you; go and find it!

Chapter One

Samuel Christopher McCubbins was an extraordinary boy. Everyone said so. Even at the tender age of ten and a half, he was imbued with such strength of character, such an aura of greatness that there could be no question that he was destined for something spectacular. Not that Samuel himself ever made mention of how incredible he was; his modesty was actually one of the most endearing things about him. In fact, if Samuel had walked around with his chest puffed out and his nose in the air uttering such nonsensical rubbish as, "pick me first, you know I'm the best," and "excuse me, but you must understand, I'm special," it truly would have ruined the effect, but of course he didn't. He didn't have to. Samuel Christopher McCubbins was an extraordinary boy, and everyone said so.

Old Lady Fusco down the street said so. She said so each and every Thursday when Samuel stopped by her house, picked up her shopping list, and brought her the groceries she needed from the corner market. He never took payment, not so much as a dime, and he always stayed long enough for tea and a chat, no matter how sunny it was outside.

Samuel's teacher said so. She said it when she saw the scores from his standardized testing, when she read his book reports, and when she graded his homework. While that was wonderful, it was the other things that she noticed that really got her attention and, as she would often tell the young, dewy eyed new teachers down in the teacher's lounge, "after 27 years of doing this it takes a lot to raise my eye." Samuel had succeeded in raising her eye, however, and had done so by raising his hand when he knew the answer to a question or when he had a question himself, helping the other students who were having trouble, keeping an immaculate desk all year round, not just at inspection time, and carrying himself with a grace and confidence Miss Pryor had yet to encounter in men three or four times his age.

Samuel's soccer coach said so, too. He said so with a slightly odd gleam in his eye, and often could be heard uttering such phrases as, "my first to go pro" and "world cup" when the subject of Samuel was discussed. Samuel was, indeed, blessed with a grace of movement and a fleetness of feet that seemed made for soccer. He seemed to know exactly where the opponent was going to kick the ball, and lead the Pleasant Valley Rockets to their first ever undefeated season, giving up only five goals out of innumerable attempts.

The girls in Samuel's school would have said so, but they could rarely stop giggling long enough to get out a word when even his name was mentioned. When he was actually in their presence, they were rendered absolutely mute. It wasn't enough that he was tall, slim, and fair of face with white blonde hair and clear, blue eyes the color of the sky on the first day of summer. It wasn't that his smile revealed a line of perfect, glistening teeth and came from a jaw that in a few years would certainly turn the corner from "well-formed" to "chiseled." No, it was that Samuel bestowed that smile, with no guile or forwardness, on the girls who were shy and spotty just as much as he did the twittering princesses. He would carry a girl's books if he happened to be walking next to her, hold a door if she happened to be following. In fact, the only black mark on Samuel's Discipline Record came from the day that he blacked Lucas Grant's eye for tripping Bella Marks and making her fall so hard that both her palms and her knees bled. Samuel got one day of after school detention for that, but secretly, the playground staff were rooting for him. Lucas had always been a bit of a bully.

Excalibur, Samuel's pet Chihuahua, would have said so, but of course Chihuahuas can't speak. If they could, though, Excalibur would have said that he loved the way that Samuel called him his "trusty steed" and scratched him behind his ears. He would have said that Samuel actually kept the promise that he made to his mother, as he held the tiny squirming puppy to his chest, and DID feed and water Excalibur every single day. Not only that, but he bathed him, brushed him, housetrained him, and taught him to sit, stay, roll over, gallop, and cantor. Best of all, Samuel snuck him in his bed at night and slipped him tidbits under the table. If forced to admit it, Excalibur would have even admitted that he loved being Samuel's steed even when it involved a homemade saddle for plastic knights and armor made out of tinfoil.

Yes, Samuel Christopher McCubbins was undoubtedly an extraordinary boy. "Such a dear," said Old Mrs. Fusco, "the brightest pupil in 27 years," declared Miss Pryor, "college scouts" grunted Coach Bob, "my light and joy" grinned his mom. You see, everyone said so.

When we first meet our hero, however, he is also a very disgruntled boy. Dusty, tired, sore, and more than a little bit frightened is our young Samuel, and with good reason. It was well past two in the morning according to the chimes winding up from the living room, and Samuel couldn't sleep. The air was musty and made his throat tickle, the bed was lumpy and broken springs poked his back in first one place and then another. To make matters worse, the glow of the security light outside looked ghostly and blue when it filtered in through the old curtains covering the window, and took the unfamiliar shapes that lurked around Samuel past benign and well into the realm of menacing. You see, Samuel was spending his first night in the section of the attic that he and his mother had spent a long and grueling week turning into his temporary bedroom, and it really was enough to leave anyone feeling disgruntled. It all began three days before, when Aunt Cathy called to speak to Samuel's mother.

Samuel was sitting at the table, eating Cheerios and staring out of the window at the beautiful day that was developing outside. So far, summer vacation had been pretty rainy, forcing Samuel to play inside, creating forts out of blankets and setting up elaborate battle scenes with his plastic soldiers. Not that he didn't enjoy those things, it was just that he'd already recreated Gettysburg, Waterloo, and Gallipoli, and was looking for a bit of a change. This day, though, was just as Sunshine Bob the Weatherman had said it was going to be, sunny and fair, with temperatures in the high seventies. Samuel had big plans for the day. He was going to begin by looking for frogs down by the creek which, after days and days of rain, was deliciously cold and frothy. Then, he was going to ride his bike down to his friend Duncan's house for some basketball with the guys. Finally, he thought he might read for a while under the apple tree, eating some early apples and throwing sticks for Excalibur to fetch. Samuel pondered these plans with delight, munching on spoonful after spoonful of Cheerios and paying no attention to the telephone conversation his mother was having in the kitchen.

All of his plans and ponderings came to a crashing end, however, when his mother clicked the telephone off with a sigh, padded over to the dining room table, sat down, and tossed a few Cheerios, dry, into her mouth. She looked at Samuel and sighed again. "Sam," she said, "you're not going to like this."

"Like what?" Samuel asked, after swallowing his mouthful and dabbing his lips with his napkin. Samuel's manners were impeccable.

"I'm going to need you to help me with something."

"Sure," Samuel said cautiously, willing as always to help, but with one eye warily on the door, the door that in a few short minutes would open to long days of freedom and leisure. He was beginning to wish he'd just grabbed some fruit to go that morning. "Can I help after I get back from Duncan's?"

His mother laughed ruefully and tousled his hair. "I wish we could wait, sweetie, but we really can't." Samuel, his full attention finally gained, looked at his mother quizzically.

"What's going on?" he asked.

"Aunt Cathy and Albert are coming to stay with us for a while…" his mother began.

"Great!" Samuel always liked Albert, even if he was a bit quiet, and the idea of a live-in-playmate sounded like fun.

"…and we're going to have to set up a bedroom in the attic."

"The attic?" Samuel said, horrified. The attic was a terrible place; cold in the winter and sweltering in the summer. There were spiders up there. Spiders and dust and who knows what else. "Why the attic?"

His mother sighed again. It seemed to be quite the day for his mother and sighs. "Well," she said, "because in a few days we're going to have more people than we do bedrooms. We need one more place for someone to sleep."

"We can't put Aunt Cathy in the attic. " Samuel said. "There's spiders up there and Aunt Cathy hates spiders."

His mother looked at him for a long moment. "Aunt Cathy isn't going to sleep in the attic." she said. "You are."

There was a moment of silence, long and thick, as Samuel stared wide-eyed across the table at his mother. His fair cheeks flushed and his azure eyes, the cause of a great deal of young female twittering, filled with tears. Extraordinary and special as he was, this was just too much. Innumerable golden hours had been dedicated, instead of to quests and adventures, to mops and bleach and cobwebs and now, now he had to give up his room? It is said that "where a man's treasure lies, there too is his heart," there are few people to whom that saying was more apropos than Samuel Christopher McCubbins. Over the years, Samuel had transformed his space from a mere bedroom to a fortress, a private place where plans were hatched and dreams were dreamed. With some glow in the dark stars and a book on astronomy that he had checked out from the library, Samuel had adorned the ceiling with his favorite constellations. Orion guarded one corner, his arrow pointing to Cassiopeia who rocked bitterly in her chair for all eternity. The big dipper hung over the bed and in the place of honor stood Sirius, the Dog Star, dedicated of course to Excalibur. On the walls, castles and trees, knights and princesses, dragons and rearing steeds moved in medieval waltz against a cerulean background. But that was just the start. On his desk sat his butterfly collection, carefully gathered and mounted over the course of years. He only collected the butterflies that had already perished, of course, and always apologized to them as he pierced their corpses carefully with a mounting pin. His bookcase was alphabetized and his soldiers separated into distinct battalions, companies, even squads and lined up accordingly. A blanket fort like none the world had ever seen, comprised of eight blankets and made into three rooms, dominated one corner. Suddenly he was expected to leave this to occupy, even temporarily, the attic?

"*Me*?" he said. "Me? Why am I staying up there?"

"Well," his mother answered, "as you said, your Aunt is terrified of spiders and even if she wasn't she... Albert will be sleeping in your room with her. She doesn't really want to be by herself right now. You understand. And, as I didn't think that *you'd* want to be her roommate," his mother shrugged as if to say "what more is there?" and, with a sympathetic sigh, left Samuel to have a well-needed pout.

Being Samuel, he soon got over such nonsense, and before lunchtime came he was upstairs with his mother, sorting through boxes of old newspapers and older photographs, moving furniture, and attacking the rafters with a broom. The next two days were despairingly similar. Move, scrub, dust, paint, repeat until dinnertime, a few dusky hours playing with friends, then collapse into bed only to start again. To add insult to injury, Samuel did in fact have to spend one miserable afternoon disassembling his fort, packing his soldiers into tins, and moving his stuffed animal collection from their treasured positions stacked on the spare bed to be stuffed callously into garbage bags and stuffed in the storage closet. Finally, though, it was done. Samuel and his mother, huffing and puffing, moved the roll away bed up the stairs and fitted it with Samuel's sheets and favorite comforter. They bought an air conditioner to put into the window, tacked old sheets to the rafters to separate Samuel's portion from the storage, and found an old bookcase into which Samuel moved some of his favorite books and knickknacks.

"There," his mother said when they were finally done. "This isn't so bad. Think of it as an adventure." And there, with the sunlight streaming in through the window and everything gleaming fresh and white, Samuel thought that perhaps, for a little while, he could.

With the arrival of bedtime, though, and Samuel's flashlightilluminated trudge up the unfamiliar staircase, he found that he could not, in fact, look upon this as an adventure. It was nothing less than a practice in misery; one that he only hoped would be over very, *very* soon. He was extremely uncomfortable. Roll away beds are not actually meant to be slept on. They are meant to have on hand so that when you're trying to be hospitable you can say, "Well, we do have the roll-away." If actually used as a bed, they must only be used for someone you most definitely do *not* want to have at your home again, because they are nothing short of a modern torture device. Also, the light and the sound were different in the attic. Was that the wind in the eaves, or some ghostly specter disturbed by the rearranging of the previous week? Was that the shadow of the coat rack, or some horrible beast, teeth and claws bared? In the gloom, Samuel couldn't be sure and he spent hour upon hour tossing back and forth, hiding his head under the pillow, and turning his flashlight on and off and on and off, becoming more disgruntled by the minute. Finally, though, exhaustion conquered fear and discontent, and by the time the grandfather clock downstairs gave three deep chimes, Samuel had drifted to sleep and, though he didn't know it, out of our story.

It may have comforted Samuel some to know that, mere feet away, his cousin also lay awake long into the night. Downstairs, under the faintly glowing forms of Cassiopeia and the big dipper, under the watchful eyes of the knights and dragons gamboling on the walls, his face tearstained and his hand clutching a worn and scuffed baseball, lay Samuel's cousin Albert, who was absolutely normal.

Chapter Two

Albert Robert Thomas Jackson was completely, totally, and utterly unremarkable. Everyone said so. Or, they would if they thought to speak of him at all, which most people usually didn't. In fact, it was only recently that Albert began suffering through the only notoriety he had ever known, being the only student in all of Greenwood Elementary to have had a parent die. One day he was talking to his Dad on a crackly telephone line, and the next – gone – just like that. Other kids had had parents get sick and go to the hospital, parents who had gotten divorced, even parents who had moved far away, but die – that tragedy belonged solely to Albert, who wished every minute of every day that he could go back in time, back to when everything was Absolutely Normal.

Before this tragedy, Albert spent his time in unnoticed mediocrity. When the class lined up, tallest to shortest, Albert was in the middle. Not down at the right, next to Sammy Sims, who could walk under his dad's Big Rig without ducking but was so fast he was a shoo-in to be the first picked for sports. Not down at the left, either, next to Luke Delgado, who was always picked second because, even as slow and lumbering as he was he was one heck of a roadblock. Right in the middle, surrounded by girls who didn't notice him either, and twittered and chattered about the other boys like Albert wasn't even there.

He wasn't unattractive, per se, though heads did not turn as he walked by. Albert had a head of brown hair, too light to be called brunette but far too dark to be called blonde. It was reddish, maybe, in the right light, but certainly not anything as exotic as auburn. "Mousy" brown some people called it, "hair colored hair" he always thought. It wasn't straight, this hair, but nor was it curly, except when it was wet. It always seemed just a little bit shaggy, no matter how short he cut it. His Dad had always teased him about it, back when he had been home and healthy enough to tease. "Are we ever gonna get this mess regulation, son," he'd ask with a chuckle, mussing Albert's head affectionately as he walked by. Albert's eyes were brown, too. Not big and dreamy, not chocolaty. Just brown. He was a little thick in the middle. Not fat like Big Nate who had to wear grown up's pants cut off at the knee. Certainly not wiry like the aforementioned Sammy, either. Just... Biggish, what his Grandmother liked to call "Big Boned," though Albert hated that, knowing full well there were no bones in his stomach.

Albert wasn't unintelligent. He was a solid B student, with some C's and A's thrown in here and there for variety. While he would always at least attempt to answer a question if asked directly, he wasn't one to volunteer information. Mostly he sat at his desk in the middle of the classroom, working on his assignments and occasionally worrying the constantly torn bit of flesh to the side of his right thumbnail. At report card time, Albert's teacher Mrs. Loch, had difficulty trying to come up with anything to write in the 'comments' section. Finally, she settled on, "pleasant, hard-working, an asset to our class."

The one area in which Albert truly excelled was baseball. He played left field and was blessed with a good eye and a better arm. Many players' hopes were dashed by the unimposing boy in left field who turned hits that people were sure would be a double or a triple at least into the end of an inning. Of course, left field wasn't the most glorious of positions, not like pitcher or first base, but it was something. Albert was pretty high up on the batting roster as well, and while he was never called on to pinch hit for someone else, Coach always gave him his shot, even when the game was close. It was his favorite sport, having been taught to him beginning at a very young age by his father, who had actually played college ball and who probably could have at least joined the minors, if he hadn't decided to do something else instead. When Albert was five, his Dad took him out and bought him his very first glove, and then showed him how to lotion it up and then bind it with a rubber band so it would form into the perfect shape for scooping balls out of the air. Every spring Albert and his Dad would get their gloves out of storage, and try them on. His Dad's always fit, of course, but if Albert had outgrown his, they'd go and get a new one the first chance they got. Two summers ago, before things got bad, his Dad had taken some leave and Albert's family had gone on vacation, all three of them, for two whole weeks. In that time, Albert's dad had taken him to a baseball game, just the two of them, and if that wasn't enough, in the seventh inning a foul ball came streaking towards them. Albert held up his glove, lovingly lotioned and shaped to scoop a ball out of the air. Not that they had any real hopes of catching it; it seemed like that part of the stadium was suddenly filled with long-armed, jostling giants, all whooping and hollering and about ten feet tall. Even so, Albert closed his eyes and held his glove straight up in the air and "plunk" the ball fell in it as neat as you please with that sweet thud only outfielders really appreciate. His dad hugged him and yelled "hold it tight, hold it tight." Albert did, he held it tight in his hand high over his head and laughed when he saw his face there on the Jumbotron. It was, undoubtedly, the single most amazing moment in Albert's young life, the memory of which carried him through many a dark time.

In Campfire Cubs, Albert did not have the most patches, nor did he have the least. He could tie a knot that held most of the time, and could paddle a canoe around the lake if he had a partner at least as apt as he was. He didn't much care for bugs, so the entomology badge eluded him, as did fire starting. Still, he dutifully attended the meetings where most of the time the cub scout leader would forget his name.

What Albert did have in common with his extraordinary cousin was that he, too, was disgruntled and he, too, had spent the previous week in the service of his mother, packing belongings into dreary cardboard boxes, some marked "Jenny's" but most marked with a word that had begun to sum up just how much everything had changed; "Storage." Albert had had the misfortune to overhear the call his mother had made to her sister who was, of course, Samuel's mom and Albert's Aunt Jenny. His mother had been sitting on the couch at the time, which was really not much of a surprise; most of his mother's days lately were spent on the couch, watching daytime talk television and smoking menthol cigarettes one after another. His mother never used to smoke, not since Albert was very young, but since his Dad died she had started again. Albert couldn't blame her, of course not, but there was a part of him – a normal part of him – that just wished that she would quit again, stop smoking and get up and maybe take a bath. Albert had suggested that she do these things. He'd also suggested that she talk to the pastor from their church who kept calling, go outside for some fresh air, and try to eat a little bit. Every time, though, the end was the same; after two or three suggestions his mother would flap one hand at him, like she was swatting at a fly. Her eyes would brim with tears and she would light another cigarette. "Enough, Albert," she would say. "I am sad, don't you see that? I'm sad and I just can't. Now go play, sweetie, go do … Something." And so Albert would go outside or up to his room, anywhere where he wouldn't bother his Mother, and be sad by himself. He also took to spending quite a bit of time in the hallway between the living room and the bedrooms, out of his mother's sight, but close enough so that he could kind of keep his eye on her. The family pictures were hung there, as well, and Albert would stare at them for seemingly endless hours, dreaming of back when his Dad was still alive, and everything was normal.

It was there, in that gloomy little hidey-hole, that Albert was sitting when he overheard his Mom call her sister, to ask if the two of them could come and stay. "I just don't want to be alone, anymore," his mother said, and Albert felt a lump rise in his throat.

"What about me?" he wanted to cry. "What about me?" Instead, he rose to his feet and went to his room, where he began to pack. It was hard to see what he was doing, though. The air conditioning, he was certain, kept making his eyes water, and the tears were streaming down his cheeks.

The packing went quickly, far quicker than Albert had hoped. Of course, all that he was allowed to take with him was one garbage bag full of clothes, and one big box to cram with all the boyhood treasures it could hold. His mother took two big bags of clothes and three boxes, something Albert found to be extremely unfair, but knew better than to challenge her. Everything else, their entire lives, went into boxes that Albert was to tape shut and label. The tape came on big rolls with a plastic handle and metal teeth; Albert's hands were sore and raw by the time the day was done, and his head was swimmy from the scent of the permanent marker. His heart ached, too, from watching everything that was familiar, was comfortable, everything that had always just been there, disappear first into cardboard boxes, and then onto a truck, carried by two big men who didn't look as if they'd care if something got broken. Albert and his mother ate dinner from Pizza Party, sitting cross-legged on a floor that still held deep dimples from where the furniture had sat for so long. They slept, what little sleep they got, on blankets and pillows strewn on the floor. Albert's mother tried to pretend that it was fun, like some sort of indoor camp-out, but deep down they both knew better and it was a relief when the alarm clock went off at 6:30 the next morning. By seven, Albert's mother was turning the key in the lock for the last time and they began their long trip to Aunt Jenny's house, where, they hoped, they could start to build their lives again.

Oh, it was miserable, that endless first day. Albert's whole body ached from the long bumpy ride, and he didn't know where anything was. He would open and shut one cabinet door after another, trying to find whatever he needed at the moment, until someone would either fuss at him or come to help. Albert's mom and Aunt Jenny sat at the kitchen table, talking, talking, talking and shooed anyone who came into the kitchen for more than a drink of water or a snack. Samuel, usually a great playmate, was acting odd, and even though he invited Albert to come along with him; down to the creek to look for crayfish, out back to work on his tree house, or even over to his friend's house to play soccer, Albert could tell that Samuel really didn't want him around. So, he took his treasured baseball and a book and went to a lonely corner of the yard to read and to think until it was dark enough to justify going to bed. There he lay, tossing, turning, staring at the ceiling, and generally pondering how life had gotten to be so miserable until finally sleep reluctantly dragged him under.

A sad boy, a lonely boy, and, before this tragedy an absolutely normal boy with nothing whatsoever remarkable about him. "A hard worker," Mrs. Loch had written. "A good kid, a decent outfielder," said his Coach. "There he is!" said the fairies at the window.

…Fairies at the window!??!

Chapter Three

"There he is!" exclaimed Moonlor the fairy with a grunt, her iridescent wings fluttering as fast as a hummingbird's as she struggled to pull her companion up onto the windowsill. "Ooooooh, there he is! There he is! Thereheis!"

Dewdron, the Leafybe that had been chosen by the King to accompany the excitable little pixie, muffled a yell as Moonlor accidentally banged his head on the bottom of the shutters yet again. In the distance, something – perhaps thunder – rumbled. Finally, his tiny fingers gained purchase and he scrabbled into the window ledge while Moonlor, her always pink cheeks blushing nearly crimson in her elation, gesticulated wildly at what Dewdron could see only to be an average-sized lump under some covers. Just then, Albert rolled over, muttered something unintelligible, and flung the blankets down around his waist, granting the anxious duo their first real look at the hero they'd been sent to collect. Not sent by just anyone, either, Moonlor and Dewdron had received this assignment, not from the Phim, or Elders, as was usually the case, but from the King Himself. The duo had stood before Him in the Throne Room and listened as the King had explained where they were to go, and why. It had been decades since they'd seen Him, but the King was as strong as always, His back straight in His carved throne, and His voice deep and even. His hands, though lined, were broad and strong and His beard, though snowy white, fell from a square chin. He was wearing his usual purple robed, embroidered with the official, Royal Seal of Gwytthenia. The Royal Seal of Gwytthenia was seven stars in a circle. In the middle of the stars was a staircase. At the bottom of the staircase was a loaf of bread, and at the top was a dove. It wasn't flashy, that seal. It didn't have dragons or unicorns or raging steeds. It was, rather like the King, Himself, unimposing yet full of power.

What the fairies remembered most about their meeting, however, was how sad he looked at the time and how much hope he had said rested on the shoulders of the hero they were to collect.

What lay before them was not, unfortunately, a very aweinspiring sight. Albert's hair was sticking up on one side of his head, and he had blanket crease across his face. He snored loudly and drooled copiously; a small puddle had already formed on the pillow where his head now lay. The two fairies, one tall (for a sprite) and one short, peered through the window.

"Are you sure it's him? Dewdron whispered.

"Well of course it is!" Moonlor snapped. "Don't be such a worrywart! He is exactly where the King said he would be."

Moonlor was determined to overcome her partner's somber nature, to lead him to see the world in the same rosy hues as she. To wit, she would berate him with names such as 'worrywart' and 'humbug' and spend a great deal of time pointing out beautiful sunsets, baby animals frolicking adorably, and such obtuse things as "the glories of eyebrows." (Moonlor greatly envied eyebrows, having none herself.) Dewdron would usually grunt, or perhaps point out that the reason she had such a rosy outlook on life was that her eyes, were in fact, bright pink. Leafybe's you see, were known for their dour insistence that pessimism was, in fact, realism in disguise.; To your average Leafybe the glass was neither half-empty nor half-full; it was destined to be spilled before it could even be drunk, and was most likely full of poison anyway.

"It's just that, well, he don't much look heroic, ye see," Dewdron was mumbling.

"I see no such thing," Moonlor snapped. "Look!" and here she reached into what was, by all appearances, a normal leather bag hanging at her side. Looks do not account, however, for whatever enchantments may be placed upon an object, and surely the crashes and bangs emitting from the tiny bag seemed to suggest that many rather large objects were lodged inside. Soon, panting, Moonlor found the object for which she had been searching and pulled it with a grunt through the bag's narrow opening. It was a map, but not the likes of which you or I are likely to have seen. Here in our world, each map serves a specific purpose and shows a specific place, and must therefore only give the briefest picture of whatever space it is depicting. A Gwytthenian map, however, must show not only latitudes and longitudes, but the sky and the heavens, and whoever may be occupying them at any time. After all, it does not do to fly through a tribe of hunting Plainsmen, unless you care to accidentally become dinner. The map must show you not only where you should go and how to get there in one world, but of many, and so miniature ethereal portals and tiny replicas of foreign worlds swirled above the surface of the map, growing larger and more detailed if they were needed, fading into the background if they were not. On this particular map, there were two lines. The first was a deep, rich purple; indicating the route that the King had outlined for them. The other, shockingly pink of course, ran parallel to the first and showed the route that the duo had taken. Both lines began at the Castle and ended at Samuel Christopher McCubbin's house, a miniature and transparent version of which hung above the map. There could be no doubt, as plain-featured as their hero may be, they were in the right place. Dewdron had no choice but to concede, and the pair duo moved forward to gather the hero their King had called. As they climbed through the window, the first fat drops of rain began to fall.

All was quiet within the McCubbin's household, save for the deep tock of the Grandfather Clock, and Albert's low snores. As silently as she could, which was quite a lot louder than Dewdron would have liked,

Moonlor began to rummage once more in her bag. She pulled out two magic wands (one holding together by only the tiniest fiber), four empty bottles, a book that Dewdron thought was entitled "Wooing Leafybes", and something that looked suspiciously like a very moldy sandwich, and, with the exception of the book which she threw in the bag so quickly that first a clatter and then the sound of something breaking rang out, she examined each object and shook her head in negation before putting it back into the bag. Albert's mother, sleeping on the bed that usually held Samuel Christopher McCubbin's stuffed animal collection, began to stir in her sleep. Dewdron's face, already lined after centuries of worry, began to look more worried still, and he made wild hand motions.

"Hurry up, ye must hurry," he mouthed, "the portal is only open for a wee bit."

Moonlor nodded and lowered her face to the bag, which magically expanded until the sprite had reached in with both hands up to her shoulders. Finally, she emerged, holding two small, corked, bottles. The first held a swirling liquid, blue and soothing. That one, Moonlor tossed to Dewdron and pointed at Albert's mother. She held up two fingers, then pointed to her own mouth. Cautiously (of course!), Dewdron uncorked the bottle and allowed two small drops to fall into the restless woman's mouth. Instantly, she settled. Dewdron left her and walked to join his partner, standing next to where Albert lay sleeping.

"Now him," Moonlor whispered. "The same."

With the first drop, Albert's snoring ceased, with the second, however, he began to drool even more; saliva now ran in a steady trickle from his mouth. He looked less heroic than ever.

"Ick," exclaimed Moonlor, wrinkling her pert little nose and sticking out her tongue, "I'm certainly not flying all the way home covered in that. C'mon," she said, "help me wrap him in his blanket."

Dewdron looked nervously at the sky. The rain that had started as they dithered outside the window was falling faster now, and every now and then he could see flashes of bluish light getting closer by the second. Also, the portal, their only way back to the world of Gwytthenia, could only remain open for a very limited period of time, otherwise they risked Mingling. Each World has its own kind of magic; when elements of one World seep unchecked into another, the effects can be disastrous. Better that it not be allowed to happen.

Outside the open window, the wind began to howl.

"We've no time for your vanity," Dewdron said. "We have to go now!" But Moonlor had already sprinkled Albert with the glittery golden powder from the second crystal bottle and was hovering above him, trying in vain to tie the corners of the comforter into a knot. Dewdron rushed to help her, making sure that he brushed against Albert so that some of the powder clung to his tiny, spotted wings. Dewdron could fly, as can all fairies, but Leafybes generally prefer the solidity of the ground and fly only short distances, and then only if it's too far to walk. Dewdron had seen more of his world, more than several worlds, than any of his kind, and was known, in fact, to be a bit of an adventuresome spirit, and yet his wings tired easily on long trips. He only hoped that Moonlor hadn't noticed. Working together, they finally maneuvered the thick blanket ends into a clove hitch, and, heaving, they squeezed through the window and into the night.

    At first, they thought that they were going to be all right. They still had time before the King had said the portal would close. Albert was secure and sound asleep. Granted, the weather was a bit less than ideal. The rain had gotten heavier, and so they were getting a bit soggy, of course, and the wind was making steering difficult, but these were experienced fairies, emissaries of the King Himself, and not easily deterred. Faces screwed against the icy drops, wings beating furiously, they flew up and up, higher and higher, towards the portal that hung open above them, spiraling in gentle circles. Portals in and out of Gwytthenia were not what one would call common, especially since the Troubles had begun. They were opened only at the will of the King, and only for special purposes. Even as an emissary, Moonlor had only seen a handful in her time. Still, if all went well and you were in the right place at the right time, they were easy enough to navigate. Zip-Zoop and you were in and out. Unfortunately, not all was going well. In fact, as the sky erupted around the trip, Moonlor couldn't help but think that things were rather unwell indeed.

Thunder crashed around them, so loud that they could feel the rumblings echoing inside their heads and chests until it was hard to think or see or breathe. The sky flashed blue-white, over and over again until their eyes stung and colors were reversed; trees stretched skeletal white arms out and the raindrops turned black. Clouds raced in from every corner of the sky, stacking one on top of the other, blocking the fairies' way home. Moonlor and Dewdron, their faces twisted in identical grimaces of effort, swerved this way and that, with Albert swinging like a pendulum below them. They rose and dove, twisted and turned, moving determinately through the deluge to their destination. They were, for once, of the same mind, working seamlessly as a team, their differences cast aside. Moonlor shouted her defiance into the sky, no flighty pixie now, this was the battle cry of a warrior of the King. Dewdron forgot that his wings were small and tired and that he preferred a cup of tea under the shelter of his Toadstool; he drove forward like a bullet shot into the sky. And no matter how fierce the wind, how erratic their flight, they never loosened their grip on the blanket with the pictures of the knights and dragons. The hero, the hope of all Gwytthenia, was in their hands and they would not fail.

They lunged through the last remaining break into the clouds, through the portal that was rapidly closing, as Dewdron in his glasshalf-empty mind had known it would, and into the darkness. They were not simply surrounded by the darkness, they were consumed.

Something, some *thing*, foreign and evil had been lying in wait for them to return. It seemed to be made of the rain and the clouds themselves. The wind rose and turned into a roar, fierce and triumphant. Unseen claws tore at the trio from every angle, unseen limbs buffeted them from all sides. By the third blow, Dewdron's wings were tattered. On the fifth, perhaps it was the seventh, Albert's blanket tore, and by the tenth the poor beleaguered fairies could hold on no longer. The trio was shattered; Moonlor was knocked far to the East and Dewdron towards the Western Sea. They spiraled, out of control, plummeting to the ground far below. Albert, still held in the air by Moonlor's shimmering powder, was tossed, blown by unseen forces towards the snow-capped mountains of the South, often referred to as "the desert of ice," a lonely, desolate land, forsaken by all creatures, except one.

Chapter Four

Albert's first awareness that anything unusual had happened, his first sensation in this new world in which he found himself, was cold. Harsh, biting cold that cut through his clothes, his skin, his muscles, all the way down to his bones. He had never had cold bones before, and discovered to his dismay that he disliked it intensely. He tried to move his right arm, and was surprised to discover that doing so hurt. His whole body hurt, in fact, was sore and tender and something heavy and frigid covered him like a blanket. He didn't remember anything horrible happening to warrant this pain, something like being struck by a dump truck or being caught under a rockslide, and yet there was no other logical explanation. To add another surreal mystery, somewhere in the distance, he could hear someone singing, a high, reedy tenor. Albert recognized the song at once, "Loch Lomond." His Mom used to sing it when he was little. Yet, it was not his mother's voice. His mother, back in the days when she sang, sang in an alto that was melodic enough, if not always precisely in tune. With difficulty, he turned his head towards the sound and his eyelids parted the tiniest slit. Bright light pierced his eyes like daggers; Albert cried out and squeezed his lids closed tightly. He tried a second time, prepared for the onslaught that was bound to occur, and was able to part his lashes millimeters farther than previously, before exhaustion and pain forced them shut. Before he could try again, though, sleep had claimed him once more.

The next time Albert floated to the surface of consciousness, his head was bumping unceremoniously along the rocky terrain as he was being dragged through the snow by his right leg, the bare foot disappearing into the grasp of someone or something Albert could not quite see. Dark had fallen, the only light coming from the myriad stars twinkling above. If he squinted, Albert could make out a vague pear shape, shadowy black in the darkness, and that was all. His head against something cold and hard, and suddenly his scalp joined the cacophony of pain screaming from various points in his body. Albert felt his body shake with shivers that were not just from the cold; his skin felt hot and feverish to the touch. He opened his mouth to ask the figure where they were, what was happening, but Albert's tongue felt three sizes too small, and his mouth was dry and sandpapery. He took in a deep breath and tried to form words. He managed only a strangled moan, more like an animal in pain than something human, before the fever pulled him under yet again.

Albert spent the next week lost in the swirling fog of fever and sickness in which he could not rest, nor could he fully wake. His skin hurt and his whole body throbbed dully. He was weak, couldn't even open his eyes or utter a word, no matter how hard he tried. His dreams were plagued by horrible things that hissed and bit, both at his body and his spirit. Voices echoed all around him; from one side, he could hear his mother; "I wish it had been you instead," she cried, and, "It's your fault." From the other, he could hear his father; "You never did hit it over the fence," his dad said, "I would have liked to see that." In the background, always, something wild growled, tried to drag him deep into the yawning abyss that spread below him. Albert fought with all of the strength in his depleted and sicknessracked body, but alas it seemed that it was all he could do to hang on and pray with a fervency generally saved for soldiers in war and parents in emergency rooms. Each time Albert felt the creature getting close, each time he began to lose hope, he would feel a smooth caress of his brow, hear a snatch of a song sung in a reedy Irish tenor, or taste a bit of broth trickled between his cracked lips.

"Keep fighting, lad," a voice said, "If the King wills it, ye'll be well soon." Somehow, that little kindness, that trickle of hope, was enough to cause the creature to relinquish its hold, at least for a moment.

One day, the voices and the growling seemed quieter, farther away, and Albert thought his shaking was less. The next day, he woke, truly woke, for the first time since he was, even though he had to make this particular discovery, snatched ingloriously and drooling, pulled through a portal, and dropped on the top of a snowy mountain. He was surprised to discover that he was ravenous; a situation magnified by the smell of something wonderful cheerfully bubbling in one corner of the room. Albert's stomach growled and his mouth was filled with eager saliva. With monumental, Olympian effort, Albert was finally able to open his eyes, though his lids were sandpapery and swollen, and take his first real look at what was most definitely not Samuel Christopher McCubbin's bedroom any longer.

For the briefest of moments, and perhaps unsurprisingly, Albert remained convinced that this was another dream, albeit one significantly more pleasant than those that had spent the past week with him in their coils. He lay on a smallish bed, piled high with cozy if rough spun blankets and pillows, and which sat in the middle of what appeared to be some sort of cottage. Thick curtains lined the walls, keeping the dwelling cozy and dim, though a slightly bluish glow seeped around the edges of the fabric, and filtered down from the curved ceiling. The cottage was dome-shaped, and immediately to Albert's front stood a small hallway with a door at the end. The hallway was cluttered with fishing gear, waders, bows and arrows and what, incongruously, a positively ancient set of bagpipes. Albert rubbed his eyes and stretched, trying desperately to either wake himself from this newest dream, or to come to terms with an increasingly perplexing reality.

To Albert's left was a series of bookcases, crammed with knickknacks, records, and the books for which they were intended. On top of one, a phonograph – complete with a large golden horn on top – balanced precariously. An ancient tapestry hung on the wall; Samuel would have known what it was at once: a family crest, known to be a sign of nobility and warriors. All that Albert knew was that it was beautiful; it was shaped like a shield, with the three points on the top made to look like snowcapped mountains, and the bottom ending in a fish's tail. A bow and three arrows crossed in the middle, in front of which was an odd looking hat with a bobble on the top. Behind all of this was a diamond shape, the top point of which was encircled by a crown. Albert's heart jumped when he saw this, though he didn't know why, and he suddenly felt better than he had in quite some time. Albert stared at the tapestry for many long moments, and would have gone on doing so if a – clearly intentional – clatter of pans hadn't drawn his attention behind him, to the kitchen from which the delicious smell was emanating and where his hero and nursemaid waited anxiously to be introduced.

Albert turned his head in the direction of the sound and saw nothing; or, at least, nothing that would have been capable of clearing its throat. He saw cabinets, a hand stitched sampler that read "Home Tweet Home" and a stove that was cleverly vented out the top of the dwelling. Albert furrowed his brow looked down low; there, he saw a small feathered bird, mostly white with a big red beak and yellow fringe flopping back over either side of its head. It was wearing a kilt of red and green, with a silver pin in the shape of three leaping fish holding it together. It was the most exquisite stuffed animal he'd ever seen, uncannily realistic. He'd had one like it for years. Well, not exactly. It was a tiger, not a penguin, but it had nearly the same amount of detail, the same wise eyes. He had known, just known, that at any moment Tigey would roar, or even speak. He'd loved Tigey more than anything, more than most people, and he'd been there for everything. His first home run; his dad's deployments, even everything that came after. His mom had thrown him away after Albert had brought him to the funeral, told him it was time to be a man. Of course, she'd apologized later and even bought him a new one online, but it was never the same. Unable to resist, Albert reached out and squeezed the penguin's soft, downy belly.

"Do ye mind?" the bird squawked indignantly, and tapped the back of Albert's hand smartly with his flipper. Albert pulled back, shaking his hand, his mouth an "O" of astonishment.

"W-what are you?" Albert asked, not so much because he thought that such a thing was the correct thing to say, simply because, faced with what seemed to be a talking penguin and lying, instead of in Samuel's bedroom, in an amazingly furnished igloo, he could think of nothing else. This was not, however, the right thing to say.

The bird, who already looked grumpy due to his downward curved beak and the ridge of feathers that met over it like a furrowed eyebrow, managed to look grumpier still. He fluffed his feathers and shuffled his webbed feet angrily. "What am I," he asked, his brogue growing thicker with his displeasure. "What am I? Well, isn't that a fine 'how ye do!' I am *who* dragged you out of the snow and ice, where I found you lying and where you certainly would have died. I am *who* has been nursing you back to health since then, wrapping your wound, feeding you broth, cooling your brow when the fevers took you. Before that, and beyond that I must say, I am an O'Cannon, the most noble of all penguin families, personal guardians to the High Lords and to the King Himself for time out of mind, known for our skill with bow and net and (if I do say so myself) bagpipes, and-"he ran out of steam, then, perhaps remembering, or perhaps realizing, that the boy spoke out of ignorance as opposed to insult. "Anyhow, that's who I am," he finished far less bombastically than when he began.

Albert gaped. "King?" he asked. "Am I in England?" Though he thought he'd have remembered hearing about talking penguins in Geography, he was relatively certain that they did not live in England.
However, try as he might, Albert could not think of anywhere else that still had such things as kings and queens.

The penguin was staring at him once again. "England?" he chirped. "I've never heard of England. I was speaking, young lad, of the Grand and Glorious High King of the Land of Gwytthenia, long may He reign."

"I've never heard of the King of Gwytthenia. I've never heard of Gwytthenia at all."

"No matter," replied Malarkey, "I'm sure that he's heard of you. It is said that He knows all of His subjects by name. Speaking of names, would you kindly tell me yours?"

Albert introduced himself, properly, the way his father had taught him. He spoke clearly, politely, and gave both his first and last name. He even included the most gloriously surreal firm handshake of his life. "And you?" he finished. The penguin hesitated. "Most call me Malarkey," he said at last. "Malarkey?" Albert said with a giggle. "That's silly!" "No, that's nonsense," Malarkey replied. "What?" Albert asked around an enormous yawn, and rubbed sleepily at his eyes. Malarkey noticed, indeed there was little that happened on the vast icy plain that he did not, and crossed to the bed. He adjusted the pillows and felt the already dozing Albert's forehead for fever. Finding none, he nodded with satisfaction.

"Alright then, young lad, young Albert, ye just sleep now, there's all the time in the world for talking." Albert slept.

Chapter Five

Each day, Albert was able to stay awake longer and longer, and he and the penguin would spend long hours together. Malarkey taught Albert to knit. For a moment, Albert pondered how the bird was able to do such a thing, lacking not only opposable thumbs but also fingers of any sort. He thought about asking, but decided he might be thought impertinent, and so turned his attention to moving the needles in the correct motions. He was surprised to discover that he enjoyed knitting. There was something immensely satisfying about turning bundles of tangled yarn into something beautiful, or, at least, serviceable. While they knitted, they talked. More accurately, Malarkey would spend hours talking and the boy would listen. It had been a long time since the penguin, gregarious by nature, had had company, and he reveled in having another to bring an end to his loneliness. Gwytthenia, Albert soon learned were Malarkey to be believed, was truly a splendid land. They were currently on the southernmost slopes, the most uninhabited of all of the lonely lands between there and the Great Castle to the north. Westward there was little but desert and The Vinelands, a wild and wooly place Malarkey explained with no little disdain. Most of civilization, in the traditional form, lay to the north and east of the castle, and on the coast of the Cerulean Sea.

One night, while the frigid winds howled outside the igloo, Malarkey told Albert a positively scurrilous tale of a time he had gone to the sea to arrest a notorious pirate captain and ended up being taken hostage on the ship instead. "And then," Malarkey finished between chuckles, "they took the poor creature and tied him to the bow of the ship as a figurehead! By the King's Name, I tried to get taken hostage again, but they wouldn't have me!" By the time the bird was done with his story, Albert's sides positively ached from mirth.

Eventually, Albert was able to stand on his own. He did so with all of the grace, dignity, and pride of an infant taking its first drunken, wobbly steps, but he did it. Both he and Malarkey breathed audible sighs of relief. Albert had, by that time, started to fixate on a vision of himself as some sort of cheerful invalid, spending the rest of his days in bed, knitting scarves that were miles long, and Malarkey, not having been able to tend to his regular chores, would often stare in dismay at his dwindling food stores or the thinness of the ice on his igloo. Therefore, they were both thrilled when their horizons broadened and their routine changed. After breakfast, Malarkey would don his galoshes and go out fishing or ice cutting. Albert would stay back at the cottage, keeping house. It became a bit of a joke between the two, Albert referring to himself as a maid and Malarkey as "Mawster" in a faux-British accent when he welcomed him home.

He soon learned how to make kelp and squid chowder from Malarkey's daily catch, and shortly after that learned to eat it without grimacing. It was actually quite tasty, if one could look beyond the ingredients. After dinner dishes were done, Malarkey would bank up the fire and the igloo would be filled with music. Sometimes, it was the phonograph that provided the melodies. Other times, Malarkey would pull out his bagpipes. Albert was overjoyed to discover that Gwytthenia had at least versions of songs that he knew from home. Loch Lomond, as he recalled from the mountain, was one of them. "Amazing Grace" was a second. Astonishingly, "Summertime,' a long time favorite of Albert's mother, had also made the transition between worlds, and the boy grew wistful just thinking about it.

One day Malarkey saw Albert eyeing the swords that lay in the corner. "I could teach you, if you like," the penguin said, nonchalant.

Albert's eyes grew wide. "You would?" he asked.

They had their first lesson that night. The sword felt large and unwieldy at first, and Albert could not find his grip. "Loose but steady," Malarkey said, again and again, "pretend it's a wee bird in your hand." This advice did not help Albert in the slightest, having never held a bird, wee or otherwise, but after a while he found his grip. After that, he took to sword fighting rather naturally, parrying

Malarkey's blows with ease, and even landing a few of his own. It was, he found to his delight, not unlike baseball in a way. Best of all, he felt his arms and his legs growing stronger.

One night, bruised and weary but supremely happy, Albert looked to Malarkey with a question in his eyes. The bird raised his eyebrows in response, the fringe dancing merrily in the firelight.

"I was wondering," Albert began. "I thought penguins," he tried again. He sighed, frustrated.

"Out wi'it, lad," the penguin replied.

"In my world, penguins spend most of their time in water. On land, they just kind of waddle. But you, you can ride horses and shoot arrows and-"

"So, was it a question you had, lad, or no?"

"Why are you so different here," Albert blurted.

Malarkey grinned. "Ah, well that's a grand tale," he said, settling back into his chair and stretching his feet, insomuch as he was able, onto the ottoman.

"My people were not always knights," he began. "Don't get me wrong, we have been for many and many-a, but once we were humble fishermen. Many are, still. The Hughes remain. And Clan Payne. One day, the most wonderful news began to spread. The King was travelling with His caravan, to bring tidings and news of the Kingdom. He was coming to the farthest reaches to see His people. Well, the village was all aflutter, let me tell ye. The tapestries were brought out of storage and beat with all the strength that could be mustered to scatter the dust of the years. The silver, long since tarnished by the salty sea air, was polished to a shine. Folks were coming in from out on the northern floes, from towns up and down the coast of the Cerulean Sea and the wee town was full to bursting. Busiest of all were the fishers. Fish were hardly plentiful that time of year, and with folks visiting from all around the fishers were working all hours. 'Twasn't the season plenty to begin with; many of the fish had gone farther south to spawn, and there was worry that we would not be able to feed all those who had come to see the King. We wanted to feast them proper, ye ken.

And so it was that two brothers were fishing by moonlight. They would each grab two corners of net in their beaks and then dive down, down and over and up. Its hard work, lad. And then when their nets were full or their lungs were empty they would swim back to their raft and leap up on it, dragging their net behind them. Well, this night those brothers had dove time and again, but their lungs were far emptier than their nets were full and they were growing tired. They stood on the raft, which was rocking gently on the empty sea; they knew there were other fishers out there, but the night had swallowed them whole. 'Once more?' the elder brother asked. 'Once more,' the younger agreed. Down they dove and up they came and still their net held only ten or so fishes.

Disheartened, they began to pull them in, when they noticed that they were no longer alone. A man stood on their raft with them. He was handsome, fair and true, and he was smiling at them. 'Having any success?' he asked. The penguins did not feel afraid. That is not to say they were unafraid. After all, finding someone, someone dry at that, on your raft in the middle of the night is a rather concerning event. But they waited for the fear to come and instead felt peace. Which is, perhaps, why instead of asking the man who he was or how he'd gotten there, they simply answered. 'Nay sir,' they said, 'we've tried with all of our hearts, but our nets remain empty.' 'Look again,' the stranger said. And so they did and their net was jumping, absolutely teeming with silvery bodies. Their beaks fell open and they squawked with joy.

As they turned to ask the newcomer how he had done such a thing, the moon came out from behind a cloud and they saw, truly saw his face. Instantly, they fell to their knees, which is no small feat for one of my kind. 'My Lord,' they said. The Prince, for that is who it was, patted their feathered heads and they grew warm all over. 'Come with me,' He said, 'and your nets shall ever be full.'

The brothers nodded, and the Prince reached into the pockets of his robes and pulled out two golden coins. On the front was the Royal Seal of Gwytthe3nis, and on the back was what would become the symbol of knighthood, a bow and arrow, crossed with a sword, both surrounded by a crown. When the brothers took them they felt a change. Their legs grew stronger, more sure, their flippers could bend in ways they never had before and, much to their delight, they fringe grew even longer and more golden. Before the Prince and the King returned to the castle, nearly all of the penguins there at the bay had entered into His service and gotten their coins, and so it remains to this very day."

Albert sais slack-jawed with amazement. "So you're saying all knights are penguins?" he squeaked.

"No, Lad," Malarkey said. "Not all knights are penguins, nor are all penguins knights. It's rare that *all* of any group or any species are any one thing isn't it?" Albert nodded.

Malarkey continued.

"For example, many goblins are cruel, selfish, and greedy but some, the line of Matta, have served as Knights of the Treasury for nigh as long as penguins have been Knights of the Field." And while penguins are, in my humble opinion, the best choice for many a task, we cannot fly. So 'tis that there are Knights of the Air. Messengers mostly, but fierce in battle. Most of those are peregrines, they call them the Kana'im, but even then all messengers are not falcons, and not all falcons are messengers. The only thing each every have in common is that the King called, and they answered."

"Do you think that's why I'm here?" Albert asked around a yawn, "the King called me to be a knight?"

"The King called you, that's for certain. Why is another question altogether." Malarkey smiled kindly at the boy's nodding head, "Perhaps a question for another day."

Albert opened his mouth to ask another question, but he snored instead.

* * *

The morning after their third fencing lesson, Albert mentioned to Malarkey that he might like to go outside. The penguin looked at him shrewdly out of his beady eyes.

"Then go," he said, "so long as ye keep the house in sight ye won't get lost."

"It's not that," said Albert. "It's, well, I don't have any shoes."

Malarkey grumbled a bit, something about "who goes on a journey without protecting his feet," and Albert, who thought of mentioning that he hadn't planned on going on a journey at all, held his tongue. In reality, the bird had been quite good to him and his occasional bouts of crankiness seemed to sprout more from a long time spent without company than any real rancor. Sure enough, the next day Malarkey was gone a very long time, and when he returned he carried two large snowshoe hares, already cleaned and gutted.

"Where did you get those?" Albert asked, for he knew enough of Gwytthenian geography by now to know that there was no other life on land, this side of the Southern Slopes.

"I went through the pass, "said Malarkey, "and on to the Northern side. By the way, it's nearly spring there, time we got you on your way. After you finish these, that is," he amended, waving the hares by their ears.

"Finish them?" Albert asked.

Malarkey grinned. "Aye, my lad," he said, "these are your shoes."

Albert, armed with a needle that Malarkey had cunningly carved out of a bone, and some sort of thick, greasy thread, spent the next few days first skinning then tanning, then cutting and sewing the hides. The roast rabbit and rabbit stew, a welcome change from the endless fish, did nothing to detract from the fact that shoemaking was a nasty and tedious task. Albert stabbed himself repeatedly with the needle, once quite badly, until Malarkey showed him how to wrap the ends of his fingers with leather. After that, the task was less painful, though not less tedious, and Albert found himself in a foul mood.

In light of that it was, perhaps, not the most ideal moment for Malarkey to broach the subject of Albert's leaving. However, penguins were known for bravery and chivalry but not necessarily for tact, and years of solitude had not improved that virtue. And so it was perhaps unsurprising that the two experienced their first real quarrel.

"I'm not ready," Albert exclaimed, his voice trembling.

"Lad, you're as fit as you're going to be lazing about the house," Malarkey replied, not unkindly.

"I've barely been outside! I. . . I've never even lost sight of the house!" Albert was getting shrill in panic.

"That will be remedied once you do it. We are in the Southern
Slopes, lad. They don't change much"

"I don't know where I'm going!" Albert retorted.

Malarkey sighed, "North, boy, the King is the only one that can help ye, He and the Prince. I know nothing about this "Earth" you mention, let alone how to get there."

"I could stay here," Albert said, hopefully.

"Nay," the bird said, sharper than he intended. "Ye can't."

"Well, you could go with me!" Albert was growing hysterical, his breath coming in short gasps.

Malarkey swallowed a couple of times and shook his head, but would say no more.

After that, the magic was gone. They still went about their routines, but it was nothing more than going through the motions. They both knew it, and the knowing hurt even more than the upcoming departure., Albert simply could not understand why Malarkey would not go with him, and the bird, well, he had his reasons but they were such that he could not even admit them to himself, let alone the boy who had come to look up to him so. The two began to grate on each other, their tempers growing shorter and their anxiety becoming larger as each day passed. Finally, as the fire roared and the aurora borealis burned overhead, Malarkey wordlessly placed a lumpy, tattered bit of cloth in Albert's lap.

"What's this" Albert said, mystified.

"It's that which ye brought with me, from wherever you came," Malarkey replied. "I thought you might like to have it when ... when ye go."

Albert reached into what had once been a blanket. He found a pillow, a small toy soldier that Samuel must have missed when he cleaned out his bed, and nothing more. Frustrated, he flopped the pillow down beside him, and was surprised when something had thumped uncomfortably against his leg. Curious, he reached deep into the pillowcase, and pulled out an old, scuffed baseball. Albert ran his fingers over the red stitching, ducking his head so that Malarkey wouldn't see the tears that rose in his eyes.

"What is it?" Malarkey asked.

Albert's lip quivered. "It's called a baseball. I caught this one day with ..."his voice hitched. "... with my dad."

"What do ye do with it?" In response, Albert tossed the ball to Malarkey. The bird caught it easily and tossed it back. There's little in life like a simple game, that act of coming together in the name of fun to lighten the spirits, and they spent the next few hours enjoying the ease of friendship before the weight of departure began to drag on them both. Malarkey listened raptly as Albert explained every aspect of the game, and even engaged in a rousing game of catch, each toss getting fancier and flashier until, that is, Malarkey fumbled the ball with his wide, smooth flippers, and it crashed through a rather ornate and expensive looking vase that sat on the mantel. With that, the magic along with the vase was broken.

"I'm sorry," Albert said quietly. The bird gazed at him, his eyes unreadable. He took a deep breath, and when he spoke it was with a harsh choking noise, as though he was trying to stop the words even as they came out of his mouth.

"Don't you think you might want to be getting to bed?" he asked.

"But I'm not tired," Albert said, yawning and rubbing his eyes.

"Even so, you'll want to get an early start in the morning." The bird looked down into his lap, not meeting Albert's eyes.

"Tomorrow?" the boy's voice squeaked. "I'm not leaving tomorrow!"

"Yes, lad, ye are," the bird said, more harshly than he had intended.

"Because I broke a vase?"

"No, because it's past time and ye know it."

"Why?" Albert whined. He didn't whine often but when he did it was rather unbecoming, especially since in this case he knew exactly why but was afraid and didn't want to say so, which made him sound not only whiny but quarrelsome.

Malarkey, though, saw the boy's heart and so instead of rising to the fight, he lay a flipper kindly on

Albert's head. "Because it's what must be done, lad. Deep down, you know it as well as me."

"But I don't understand! You could at least go with me!:"

"This again!" The bird was obviously flustered. "I said I canno' go with ye. I don't need to tell you my reasons! But I can tell you when it's time to leave me house!"

Tears rose in Albert's eyes, but finally, he nodded. Unwanted, again. He supposed he should be used to it. He grasped Malarkey's hand for a moment, fiercely, and then went to sleep.

Neither man nor beast slept much that night, each too proud to say what was on his mind or to let the other see how hurt he was. It was a silent night, and a dreary morning as Albert packed a satchel with a few supplies and his fewer belongings – the baseball, the chanter that Malarkey had given him one happy night around the fire, and the few scraps of blanket that had still clung to him when Malarkey found him in the snow. Then, with one last backward glance, set out into the brightness and the unknown.

Chapter Six

It was an easy enough walk, even for a scared young boy with a heavy heart. The pass between the two tallest peaks of the Southern Slopes was easy to see, and the ice and snow were packed tightly, as easy to walk on as a forest path as long as you could avoid the slippery spots. Albert trudged along, his head down against the glare of the sun, his shoulders slumped, his baseball clutched in his hand for comfort. Around about noon, Albert decided that then was as good of a time as any, and perhaps better than most, to stop for lunch. Cold fish is, unfortunately, an acquired taste, and one that Albert had not yet acquired and yet he nibbled gamely on, gazing at the landscape around him. Lonely as he was (it's amazing how quickly one can get used to the company of another, especially if it's good company), and regardless of the butterflies that still flittered nervously in his stomach (until recently, Albert's idea of a good adventure was putting both ketchup *and* mustard on his French fries) it was difficult to stay despondent in the face of such beauty. The sun was glinting off of the ice on the mountains, sending back rainbows of color and every now and again a bird would soar by overhead, crying "scree" into the ether. The scree would bounce back and forth, echoing off of the mountains in eerie harmony, and after a while, Albert thought it might alleviate the loneliness if he could hear another voice, even if it was a mountainized version of his own. Swallowing the last of the cold fish pie with effort, he rose to his feet, brushing bits of slush and gravel off of the seat of his pants.

"Hello," he bellowed. Original it was not, but magical nonetheless as the rocks sent the sound back to him. "Hello. .. ello. .. ello. . loooo." He tried a couple of other words and, because he was an eleven-year-old boy and an absolutely normal one at that, it's possible that one of them was a just slightly coarser way of saying one's sit-upon. The echoes dutifully complied with both that and the gales of laughter that followed, which, of course, made him laugh even harder. Once he had worn that joke out quite thoroughly, Albert began down the descent, singing "Take Me Out to the Ballgame," gustily and in an almost perfect round.

He had gone roughly fifty yards when he tripped over a tiny ridge of stone, disguised as a shadow that caught his toe. He windmilled his arms wildly, desperately searching for a handy and helpful outcropping of rock that he could use to steady himself, but there were none. Albert tumbled, head over toes, barking his elbow on one boulder and cutting his scalp quite badly on another. Sky and stone, snow and ice changed places at an alarming rate as Albert's body contorted. He managed to kick himself in the back of his own head, something he would have believed to be patently impossible, before coming to some sort of rest, if not stop, on his belly. Prone, he slid, scraping along the scree before landing painfully on a ledge far below where he began and far away from the path. Though Albert would not have believed it at the time, he was rather lucky. A few feet in either direction or he would not have landed on the edge, but rather continued his downward progression another hundred feet or so until he found the river with what would have certainly been a splash of finality.

Albert did not, in fact, believe himself lucky. The rocks were sheer on either side of him, too steep for him to keep his feet. When finally he worked up the courage to worm his way to the edge of the plateau and peer over, the sight of drop, straight down for what seemed like miles to a foamy river far below, stole his breath from his lungs and made his head feel swimmy. He pushed himself away and scrambled backwards until his back was pressed against cold but solid rock. At this moment, overwhelmed and overtired, Albert did something that was absolutely normal. He put his hands in his arms and cried as he hadn't in years, not even when his father died. He cried as a child; loud, noisy sobs that left him with a scratchy throat and mucus running down his face. He cried until he could cry no more. He cried until the sun began to sink. It grew even colder as the afternoon faded. Albert's pajamas, sufficient enough in the comforts of a home, if not his home, offered very little protection. He found himself wishing that, if he had to be yanked out of his world and into this, that it had happened when he were a bit more presentable. Albert wrapped the thin blanket, the red and green of the O'Cannon's of course, around his shoulders. He hated that blanket. In that moment, and he was rather ashamed to it admit it, especially later, he hated the bird who had given it to him even more. Albert huddled up, and waited for whatever was to come.

About the time that Albert was pinwheeling down the mountain, Malarkey was engaging in quite the spirited argument with himself, and losing. The top layer of his thoughts were firmly convinced that he did the right thing, and told him so, loudly. He had made a promise, if only to himself, never to return from these mountains. He'd made a vow, if to no one in particular, that he would not speak, not for the rest of his life, to any citizen of Gwytthenia. Promises were made and, regardless of to whom they were made or the circumstances in which he had made them, they were not to be broken. Of course, the thoughts at the top of our head, the ones that scream the loudest, are often false. Any wise creature knows this and Malarkey, for all his faults and foibles, was a wise creature indeed. And so the small still voice inside him did not relent, no matter how loud the others may be. He had made different promises as well, the tiny voice said. Promises to guard. Promises to protect. "Those were different," the loud voices said, "I was little more than a wee child, then." "Were you?" the quiet voices countered, "Or are you acting childish now?"

Back and forth, parry and thrust the voices went until Malarkey was pacing, his feet slapping against the floor. He muttered quietly, and tiny feathers began to molt from just behind his fringe. It was in the midst of this cacophony that a block of ice fell from the roof with a crash. Later, Malarkey would swear that he'd replaced that block just recently. That he had, in fact, repaired all of the loose or thinning blocks in the igloo. However, repaired or not the fact remained that the block was in tiny, dagger-like shards on the floor and sunlight was streaming into the domicile unencumbered. The sunbeam fell in a perfect rectangle, diagonally from ceiling to mantle and from that humble wooden shelf something was reflecting bright and gold. Squinting, Malarkey walked over to investigate. The golden light came from a coin, tucked behind the effluvium of sentiment and practicality, and it sat among a thin scrim of dust, Malarkey could not easily reach back quite that far. He strained and stretched and brought the coin down. The King's face stared back at him, and with his heart galloping, Malarkey remembered the day, that glorious day, in which the King had given him both the coin and a Knighthood. The top voices started to scream again; for such memories brought the kind of pain that could barely be borne, but Malarkey hushed them, and stared into the King's eyes. "All right, then," he muttered. "All right," and hurriedly he began to pack.

    The sun had long since disappeared, and Albert sat listening only to the chattering of his teeth and the crashing of the water below. The moonlight was tricky; it cast shadows that moved and lunged and he had startled so many times that he simply had no adrenaline left. Thus, when he heard a dull thud right behind him, he never moved. "Boy!" a thin, reedy voice called above him, but Albert snuggled more deeply into the blanket, rubbing at grainy eyes and shaking himself out of what he thought must have been a dream. "Lad!" the bird called again, and this time Albert looked around wearily.

Behind him hung a rope, thick and full with the salty tang of seawater. It came from a ledge high above, a ledge from which Albert could first see only the blue bobble of a hat that he knew well, and then the hat itself, and finally the white face and curved beak of his friend, come to rescue him once again.

It was a long climb back up the rope, one that Albert would not have been able to make just a few weeks before. But, Malarkey and some other, indefinable force, had been caring for him since then, and though he struggled and twice almost slipped, he made it. Once up there, he was finally able to do what he'd wanted to do since for many days. He got down on one knee and wrapped his arms around Malarkey, holding him tight. Malarkey's flippers wrapped around the boy's waist and they stood like that for a long while. Albert's eyes travelled to the large bundles that the bird had brought with him, bundles filled with ropes, blankets, food, even a bow and arrow and two fine swords.

"You'll stay with me, then?" Albert asked.

"All the way to the end," Malarkey replied. "All the way to the end.

Chapter Seven

They waited together, neither able to sleep, until light once again graced the path, at which time the duo started down the mountain. The descent was quicker and more uneventful than Albert could have imagined; Malarkey knew the shortest and safest paths and his webbed feet guided Albert unerringly down. There were a few places where rockslides had rendered the path unusable, leaving vast drops and chasms. At these, the duo once again looked to the rope, repelling one after another. Albert's arms soon burned and felt alarmingly rubbery, but somehow he was able to hold on, though he never did master the rapid hand over hand motion that the bird used. Each time, after reaching solid ground, Malarkey would untie the anchor knot with a quick twitch of the rope. It was a neat trick, one that Albert never could master, no matter how he tried.

There were ever-increasing signs of life as the terrain began to flatten. Wildlife trails and prints gave way to caves and then to burrows; there were even a small number of leaning, weather-beaten shacks. Albert was curious about the dwellings and wanted to linger, but

Malarkey moved by them quickly, almost scuttling and looking nervously side to side.

"Can we stay there?" Albert asked, "Just to rest?"

"Nay lad," Malarkey replied, hustling him along, "those are not for us."

Albert's brow furrowed. "But they're empty," he exclaimed.

Malarkey said nothing, but shook his head quickly from side to side. "I don't see anything."

"And ye may not, not until it's too late. These are harsh lands, haunted, some say. Stories tell that the souls that perish, trying to scale the slopes, never leave. They can't you see, their bodies are under the snow and rock. So those houses were built as a place for them to rest." "Ghost houses?" Albert asked incredulously. "Those are ghost ... apartments?"

"Quietly now,' Malarkey said by way of reply, and they hurried away.

As the sun was beginning to get frighteningly near the horizon, they came, finally to the lush green growth of a riverbank. The river itself was a jolly-seeming thing, rushing and burbling over the rocks as it wound to and fro through the valley. Both Albert and Malarkey drank thirstily, splashing the chilly water onto their faces and necks, and then they each set themselves to the tasks necessary to bedding down for the oncoming night. Malarkey caught some trout fresh from the river and Albert rustled around the underbrush and found some berries; round and plump, their skin an enticing rosy orangeish color, they made Albert salivate. He brought back many handfuls of them, carrying them in a pouch made from his shirt, and Malarkey pronounced them not only fit to eat, but an actual Gwytthenian delicacy. The duo ate them by twos and threes, the sweet juice running down their chins, while the fish roasted on a spit over a roaring fire. After dinner, they settled in around the flames. They were quiet for a minute, their minds wandering over the events of a very long couple of days. No more than a moment after that, they were asleep.

Dawn broke, early and crisp, and brought with it a barrage of birdsong, mostly originating from fowl the likes of which Albert had never heard before. In addition to the common songbirds that we have here, warblers, robins, sparrows and the like, there were also Mailais – a living rainbow with long, dangling plumes, Canns – large fisher birds not unlike our pelicans, if one could overlook the two heads, and the bright, twittering Emis, not to mention a fezzant or two to be sure. This group, singing their morning salutation to the sun, woke the duo sleeping by the embers of the fire. Boy and bird yawned in unison, stretching as the stiffness of a night spent on the ground began to leave their bodies, and together they began tending to the necessary preparations to begin their day. Malarkey caught some more fish for breakfast, something that Albert had begun to like a bit after his times in the hut and which tasted fantastic when compared to an empty belly, while Albert himself stoked up the fire. After the flames began to flicker orangely, he started to pack their belongings into the neat traveling rolls that Malarkey had taught him, and the bird himself rummaged along the riverbank for some more berries. Finally, they were ready to begin.

They decided, after a brief debate, to travel northwest along the river for a day or two. The mountain path had taken them farther east than they had planned, and every day spent by the river was a day in which they did not need to deplete their stores. Thus, they chased their shadows as morning passed, chattering companionably about this and that. The unpleasantness that had been between them had passed like a cloud before the sun, and both seemed resolute in their desire to not mention it again. And so they focused on trivialities, stories of jousts at the castle and horrible teachers at school. Albert was astonished to discover that penguins at least had to attend school just like their human counterparts. Step after step and word after word they had covered roughly five miles from their first campsite, and they saw the first patch of what they would come to call "the blight"; spongy, foul-smelling bogs that were black and rotten in the middle and a sickly yellow along the edges. While unpleasant, the patches were, at first, unremarkable, a thing at which to wrinkle one's nose and to move carefully around. Albert, still ignorant of what was considered "normal", assumed that they were simply another part of this ever-increasingly odd situation in which he found himself. It wasn't until after lunch, just as Albert was trying to get up the courage to ask that they stop for the day when they saw the third patch, oozing as far as ten feet from each of the riverbanks, , that even Malarkey was unable to hide his concern. Albert, spying the furrow between his companion's feathered brows, spoke.

"What is it?" he asked in a whisper, governed suddenly by an impulse to keep quiet that he couldn't quite explain.

Malarkey replied, his voice low as well. "I've no idea," he said. "It's unlike anything I've ever seen before, and, in truth, I don't care much for it. I think that we should stay as far away from it as possible."

"To the north, then?" Albert asked, motioning to his right, where the trees thinned and the riverbank turned to gently rolling hills. Plains, beige with some sort of waving grain, were barely visible on the horizon.

Malarkey paused, considering, and then shook his head. "Tomorrow, I think," he said. "The plains are a lonely place, and we should be hard-pressed for anything fresh before long."

Late afternoon, when the sun was turning the peculiar shade of gold that let one know that while sunset had not yet begun it would do so rather quickly, they came around a river bend and saw what Albert first believed was a goat. It had the legs of a goat, anyway, grey and furry, and they bent backwards at what looks like the knee but is actually the ankle. He had the horns of a goat as well, ridged black horns that curled back and around. However, Albert had never before heard a goat mutter "drat" in exasperation before. Then again, he'd never known a penguin that could wield a sword or play a tune and so, even when he heard the second "drat" it did little to convince him that he was wrong in his presumption.

However, when Albert stepped on a stick, cracking it under his foot, the creature stood up, on two legs. Albert looked up, and up, and up, past a floppy, burgundy vest and a long black and silver beard to a rather human face.

"Oh!" the creature said, "it's you!"

Albert took a step back. "H-have we met?" he stammered.

"No!" the beast said with a wink, "but I'm not wrong am I?" Still craning his head backwards, his mouth open in a small "o", Albert shook his head.

At his side, Malarkey let out a quick snort of disgust. "A satyr," he trilled, "shouldn't you be out in the Vinelands with the rest of your sort."

"A penguin," the satyr retorted, no less cheerfully than before. "Shouldn't you be up North with yours?"

Malarkey looked at his webbed feet. If he had teeth, he would have been gritting them, but as it stood he only clacked his beak ever so slightly.

"Well then, that's settled," the Satyr said. "And to answer your question, no. Revelry, spirits, nymphs, I'm far too old for those sorts of shenanigans," he shuddered, "retired, one might say, the only vices left to me are a good pipe in the evenings and a good nap whenever the mood strikes, which is rather often if I do say so myself. In fact

I'm *pining* for a nap right now," he leaned against a furry needled tree and paused expectantly.

Albert and Malarkey remained silent and the Satyr shrugged. "Because it's a – never mind. Oh well, not for everyone, humor. And with that out of the way, Zeek Elmshade, at your service." He bowed low, his horns level with Albert's face and his hands, human hands on human arms, thrust jauntily out to the sides."

Albert smiled then. Malarkey's obvious displeasure notwithstanding, Zeek was clearly a jolly old soul and though he seemed a bit intimidating, what with the horns and the legs and whatnot, Albert couldn't help but like him.

"I'm Albert," he said, and this is Malarkey," and then he blurted, with no planning whatsoever, "I like your legs." Immediately his ears turned quite vermillion and he fought the urge to smack himself in the forehead.

The satyr's browed furrowed for a moment, but his smile remained. "Thank you," he said, "I grew them myself. I rather enjoy yours as well. Colorful."

Albert blushed as he looked down at his pajama pants. Zeek continued. "Now, if you don't mind me asking – you seem a bit if you don't mind me saying, not from around hereish so, is it you who is creating this ick and if so would you please stop? It's hurting my friends, you see, and I can't seem to fix it." "The ick?" Albert asked.

"Yes," Zeek said matter-of-factly. "Maybe you don't call it that. Maybe you have a different name. Names are funny things after all. For example," he waved a hand in one direction, "you might call that tree an oak and that one," another motion,"a willow and you wouldn't be wrong per se. I myself call them Grandfather and Serena, them being my friends and all, but no matter what you call the ick I fear it would still be ick and I do not like it."

"Oh," Albert said in understanding. He pointed at the blackened ooze. "I didn't make that. I don't like it either. It's creepy."

Zeek looked at him, considering, and tapped his mouth with one finger. "Creepy. To creep. To move stealthily and sneakily, often to no good purpose. Yes, that's a good word for it, I like that word very much. Suitable. Please watch closely."

With that, Zeek walked to the tree that he'd called Grandfather and reached far above his head, farther than Albert would have been able to reach with even a boost, and cupped his hands around a small twig that had broken in half and was hanging by only a tiny bit of bark. The satyr murmured something softly, and when he removed his hands the twig was whole once again.

"And this," he leapt to a flower that Malarkey had accidentally trodden upon, its blossom drooped forlornly to the ground and some petals lay fallen. A brush of his hand and the bloom nodded proudly once again.

"And this" he bounded over Malarkey's head, the bird let out a squawk of indignation, Albert felt himself growing slightly dizzy. Zeek snatched at the grass, and Albert saw, crawling in his hand, an iridescent green beetle that was doing its best to crawl with only five working legs. A moment later, and the sixth leg was working again.

"It's what I do," Zeek said by way of explanation. "I fix hurts. But this," he fell to his knees and plunged his hand in the blackened ooze, "This isn't a hurt. It's just wrong. I can fix hurts, but I can't fix wrong." He looked down, forlornly. Albert's stomach chose that rather inopportune moment to growl loudly and he clasped his hands over it in embarrassment. Zeek grinned. "Now that," he said proudly, "that I can fix." The satyr rose to his feet once again, wiping the ick on his already stained tunic. "I would be honored if the two of you would join me for dinner."

Chapter Eight

Zeek strode off through the woods, his long legs covering yards at a time and effortlessly maneuvering over roots and stones. Albert had to jog to keep up, and Malarkey looked and sounded like a wind-up toy, his feet flapping furiously as he wheezed and muttered. Eventually, they found themselves in a little glade that seemed, in a way that Albert could not quite put his finger upon, like a house. The grass and clover were still grass and clover; you could watch them blow in the breeze, feel them if you knelt and ran your hands over them. Yet, if you looked at them with just your peripheral vision, they became a carpet. There was a large, moss-covered branch that became a bed, and a couple of stumps masquerading as chairs. Zeek spread his arms and smiled warmly. "Welcome to my home. Please make yourselves comfortable. Dinner will be in just a moment."

While Albert sat cross-legged and marveled over the carpet that wasn't, Zeek reached into a leather pouch at his waist and pulled out a small lyre. He placed it in the crook of his arm just as Malarkey finally caught up to them and flopped to his back, his chest heaving. Music filled the glade, bringing with it chargers piled high with food.

Albert's eyes widened. He saw s'mores, pizza, apple pie. With a yell of delight he picked up a goblet; filled with icy fizzing soda pop, and guzzled it down in one swallow followed by an enormous belch.

"Sorry," he said, blushing, his hand over his mouth.

"You're welcome," Zeek replied.

Malarkey, meanwhile, was dipping his beak into a large tureen of an aromatic creamy soup. "This is fish chowder!" he cawed. "It's me mum's fish chowder. I've never had nowt like it. How did you do this?"

Zeek shrugged. "I fix hurts," he said simply. "Few things fix hurts quicker than favorite foods."

Malarkey smiled at him then, tentatively. Zeek raised his chin in acknowledgement, and they all fell to. A half-hour later, Malarkey was scrubbing furiously at his face, trying to remove the last sticky bits of marshmallow from his first, and last, disastrous taste of s'more. Their stomachs were distended, and their hearts were full. A good meal, especially the right kind of good meal, can do that. A mother, making chicken soup for her child who his home with the 'flu knows this. A father, cutting waffles into squares and triangle using his "special secret technique" knows that. Zeek knew it as well, and gazed contentedly at his new friends.

"How long as the ick been here?" Malarkey asked.

Zeek sighed. "Too long," he replied, "a couple of years, but it's gotten much worse as of late."

"What have you seen?"

"Seen?" Zeek said, "I stay in my glade with my friends. I keep them safe. I can tell you about the Brownies that live among the toadstools, and the great stag who was once a fawn with a broken leg. But beyond this wood I have not seen much, not for a long time. But heard? I have heard many things. Listening. That's another way to fix hurts."

"Well then, what have you heard?" Albert pressed. The sky was turning dusky.

Zeek strummed on his lyre again and waited before answering. Slowly, lights began to flicker in the glade. Lavender, blush pink, sky blue they danced and shimmered. One of the lights, yellow like a candle's flame, drifted near and Albert held out his hand. The light landed, pulsing softly. Albert looked closer and saw,
underneath the light, six small legs and a tiny face smiling up at him. Albert smiled back and the light-creature. . Bug?. . Sprite?. . .drifted off again.

Once the clearing was aglow, the satyr spoke. "I've heard stories of fearsome creatures like none any have ever seen. I've heard of renegades ambushing travelers. Of whole tribes that deny the King."

The satyr wiped at his eyes, and Albert saw that he was crying. Without thinking, Albert crawled over and hugged Zeek. Zeek hugged him back tightly, but spoke over his shoulder to Malarkey. "Our beautiful world is wrong, Sir Knight. Not hurt, but wrong. Can you help it?"

Malarkey poked at the ground with a stick. "I'm retired, in a sense, as well," he said. "Have been for longer than the lad has been alive. I fear I cannot help. I think, though, that I'm beginning to know who can." The pair shared a meaningful look over Albert's shoulder as they nodded. Albert did not notice, for the moment, and that was probably for the best.

A short time later, Zeek offered to make up a couple of beds for his guests. It was on the very tip of Albert's tongue to accept, but his words were interrupted by an enormous yawn and while he sat there, his mouth hanging open, Malarkey spoke.

"We cannot, friend. We have miles yet to go, and perhaps less time than we believed."

The satyr's shoulders slumped, but he nodded. "I'll walk you back to the path," he said.

The lights followed them, closely enough that Albert, yawning again, almost swallowed one. When they were back on the path, Albert hugged Zeek again and Malarkey shook his hand.

"Well-met, Satyr:" he said.

"Well-met, Sir Knight," Zeek replied.

Malarkey ruffled his feathers indignantly. "As I said, I'm retired," but Zeek shushed him, holding one finger to his own lips and winking.

"You'll see," he said, and with that he turned and left. Four long strides later he was out of the sight. Malarkey turned to Albert.

"To the North?" Malarkey asked. "Most definitely," Albert replied.

"Can you?" Malarkey asked.

"I think I'd better."

The duo turned to their right, towards the north, and though many miles lay between them, towards the King who was awaiting their arrival. They stayed as far from the stream, and thus the poisonous illness that it seemed to spawn, as they were able while staying true to their course. Though their stomachs rumbled and churned, the pair moved quickly, covering several miles before the sun began to sink downward on their left. The lush, green riverbank had turned to sparse forest, and then to rolling fields thick with clover and wildflowers. Ahead, the prairies were becoming more and more visible. Still in sight, though mercifully at a good distance, the small toxic stream burbled forlornly to itself. It was only when the fields around them turned from blood red with the light from the setting sun to dim and purple that Malarkey suggested they stop. Albert, exhausted beyond all measure, did not reply, simply slipped his pack onto the ground with a thump, and slid promptly down beside it, so hard that his teeth clacked in his mouth.

"Too dry for a fire," the bird said, running the grass between his flippers. It was green still, but brittle and high. "We could dig a pit," he continued.

"Too tired for a pit," Albert mumbled, his arm thrown over his eyes. Malarkey, though wary of the thought of night in an unfamiliar field without the flickering protection of a fire, was every bit as weary as his companion, could feel the exhaustion all the way down to his bones, and so it was with no great hesitation that he too flopped down upon the hard ground as the first stars began to appear high above them.

Chapter Nine

Albert, one would think, would have fallen asleep immediately; he himself was sure that such would be the case. Instead, he lay awake with his hands folded under his head, staring at the strange constellations. Albert had learned a little bit about the placement of the stars while he was on a camping trip with the Boy Scouts, and he began looking for the few formations that he remembered. The Big Dipper should be somewhere; so should Orion, forever preparing to shoot an arrow across the sky. They were not there, either of them, nor was the North Star, Venus, or anything else that Albert could recognize.

The ground was rough and lumpy, and the roots of a tree with odd, star shaped leaves and gnarled branches were sticking him right in his hip, no matter which way he lay. He heard, not the sound of whatever television show his mother had fallen asleep to, but the occasional hoot of an owl – at least he thought it was an owl, and the bubbling of the water nearby. It was there under that strange sky that Albert felt the first sucking wave of homesickness. It was surprising, in fact, that he had not felt it before then, whisked away as he had been. However, there had first been the business of getting well, and then the delicious task of exploring this new land. Besides, home had not been home to Albert since his father died. Still, though, at least parts of it were familiar. Here, even the stars were not the same. Albert missed his mom, he missed his room with the oak tree that tapped against his window on breezy nights, and he even missed the long hours trapped in a desk at school. He missed baseball games and video games, and the Top 40 playing on the radio.

As Albert started thinking about music, the strangest thing happened. It seemed that the wind itself was singing. A haunting, sweet melody came out of the west, low and barely audible. When the wind blew, the music grew louder. Albert sat up and looked around, but could see nothing. He thought, for the briefest moment, about exploring for a bit, to see if he could find the source, but the night pressed blackly over unfamiliar terrain. Instead, Albert lay back, and let the music sing him to sleep. If it were still there, he would explore in the morning.

It was, in fact, still there. The music was actually a bit louder and more cheerful; a bouncy tune that made both Albert and Malarkey tap their toes to the beat. They hummed as they broke down camp, wordless tunes that rose and fell with the voice on the wind. At Malarkey's insistence, the pair set out due North, instead of looking for the source of the sound. Albert wanted to quarrel, but he found that he could not. To quarrel would take his attention away from the music, and that was a thing he felt he must not do. It was, it seemed, a moot point for as the day went on, they found themselves edging more and more west, as if the music itself was pulling them. They would correct themselves, turn back towards the prairie with the sun on their right, and soon they would be chasing their shadows once again. Soon, they were surprised to find themselves back at the river. The ick was worse than ever, crawling thick and black away from the banks. Albert and Malarkey walked along the very edge, wrinkling their noses at the foul smell and looking away from the poor animals that had gotten caught in the fetid ooze. Gradually, unknowingly, Albert and Malarkey began moving faster and faster still. Before long, they were running, panting in unison as Malarkey's webbed feet comically slapped the grass. They covered one mile, and then two, and Albert's cheeks glowed rosy with effort.

"Need ... a drink," he panted.

"Aye," Malarkey replied, but neither stopped. The music moved faster as well, a wordless wailing rising and falling to a frantic beat that called "to me, come to me, faster, faster."

As they drew close to the source of the sound, Albert and Malarkey could feel the rhythm pounding in their ears and their chests, dreadful and insistent. They cleared the top of a small hill, and finally they could see it, a small rocky cave, and the first emissary of the mountain range that lay far to the west before the deserts. The stream and the music both flowed from the opening of the cave, and the blight was the worse that they'd seen. It was everywhere, coating the rocks slickly, covering the trees. The branches had bent and twisted under it, and in the knots in the trunks Albert thought he could see weeping, groaning faces. The ick was even in the air here, a dense fog that pulsed to the beat and formed itself into strange visions, nightmares. Albert saw in it his mother, crying and alone, and he saw his father laying skeletal and lethargic in a hospital bed. He even saw himself, as from above, broken and dead on the icy mountains of this foreign land. Nor was he alone. Malarkey saw his parents as well, sobbing and weighted down with shame. He saw the gates of the Castle closing, at least for him, forever. He saw the King, His eyes filled with sorrow as Malarkey was drug away from Him.

"We need to leave," Malarkey said, backing way and tugging on Albert's arm. "Now, boy. This place is evil."

Albert stood, immobile, saying nothing. When Malarkey looked over at him, he saw in horror that the boy's eyes were blank, unseeing. The music swelled, drawing Malarkey's attention unwillingly back to the cave. His pupils began to expand and contract, expand and contract in time with the endless, hypnotizing beat. Like something malicious and alive the fog reached out to him with shifting tentacles. He resisted for a moment, fought the pull with all of his might. He tugged and pulled, screamed and shook his head until his fringe of feathers danced as well. He closed his eyes tightly against the fog, but his efforts were futile. In a matter of seconds his eyes were blank as well, and the duo moved slowly and stiffly, as sleepwalkers, into the muck.

The black ooze pulled and sucked at their feet, making moist pops every time they took a step, and wherever it touched their skin the flesh turned red and itchy. The foul smell filled their lungs and the music filled their heads, yet they moved inexorably forward, towards the mouth of the cave and their doom. Suddenly the music stopped. Everything, in fact, stopped. The birds above did not sing. The branches of the trees did not rattle and whisper in the breeze. Even the creek seemed to still. The only sound that Albert could hear in the face of that heavy, waiting silence was his blood pounding through his veins.

With a roar that made Albert's eyes water, that seemed to split the sky itself a creature leapt from the mouth of the cave. As soon as its feet landed with a thunderous crash, the creature began to grow. What fit through the mouth of a rather mediocre cave suddenly filled
Albert's entire line of sight, eclipsing all else. "Oh, but it's beautiful," Albert thought, bedazzled. He was not incorrect. The body was draconic; Albert bit back a hysterical giggle as he was certain at one point he had a dinosaur toy that exact shape. Every scale on the Chordra's skin was perfectly uniform in size, shape, and color and they marched in glorious conformity up and up. At the shoulders the neck split into numerous heads. Minotaurs,

dryads, foxes, gnomes all grinned manically, their faces in rictuses that were somehow both smiles and frowns. Their eyes shined eerie gold, the lids unblinking. Deep claws scored the earth as the creature began to dance. Right, left, stomp. Right, left, stomp. Unwittingly, Albert mimicked his motions, his feet slurping in the muck. Opening its myriad mouths, the Chordra began to sing:

> *Come with me, come with me,*
> *To the pools of popularity*
> *Where comfort is conformity,*
> *Eternally..*
> *Once numb with me, your fears resign,,*
> *Let your thoughts entwine with*
> *mine Trade woes in life for death*
> *divine.*
> *You can't decline.*

Malarkey's entire body shook with effort as he visibly fought the hypnosis that had overtaken him. As his eyes cleared, he threw himself to the ground, rolling out of the monster's grasp.

"Your sword," he squawked. "Albert, draw your sword!"

Albert did not. Fully under the control of the beast, he only swayed slightly, half-moaning a negative, "Nnnnnnooooo, nnnnnoooooo," as the Chordra bore down upon him.

Malarkey rushed to save his friend. With a battle cry that rang out for miles, he jumped between Albert and the creature, yanking at the sword, twice as big as the bird himself, which hung from the boy's belt. On the third attempt it came free, swinging in a high arc that severed one of the singing heads of the Chordra. With that, the song became dissonant, harsh and buzzing. Albert shook his head to clear it, catching the sword that Malarkey heaved as the beast attacked once again. Albert dodged and thrust, not even trying to remember all of the things that Malarkey had taught him in their training sessions on the ice, but instead moving solely for survival. Had they the time, which they most definitely did not, Malarkey would have explained that this was the best way to fight: those who pondered overlong were often not around to ponder another day. Be it beginner's luck, the lessons of a great teacher, or the hand of the King ,Himself, it worked, and by the time Malarkey had reentered the fray, another of the creature's heads lay on the ground. Visibly weakened with a thick, viscous fluid pouring from its various wounds, still the Chordra advanced. Moving in the seamless synchronization usually found in men who have fought next to one another long and hard, the duo moved to flank the beast. Jumping in unison, they severed two of the remaining heads. With a thunderous crash, the creature fell forward, and the ground trembled under its weight. With a roar coming from his throat and bloodlust in his eyes, Albert charged forward.

Should anyone from our world have seen him in that moment, it was doubtful that they would have recognized him, so different was he from the mild-mannered boy they knew. His sword slashed one final time, and the creature was dead.

Albert stood, panting, and staring at the slain monster. Suddenly, the enormity of what had happened struck him. His sword fell from trembling hands and he sat down hard. The boy held still for a few moments, his head in his hands. Once he had composed himself, which took an admirably short time, he began to look around for Malarkey. The penguin stood, still as a statue, and staring with a statue's unfeeling eyes. Fearing that he was hurt, Albert ran to his friend, and knelt down beside him. He began running his hands over Malarkey's slick feathers, feeling for a wound, and calling his friend's name. It was then that he noticed that Malarkey was muttering something over and over again. Albert put his ear to the curved beak, trying to decipher the words. It took several repetitions before he could understand what the bird was saying.

"Courage," he was whispering, over and over. "It wasn't lost. Could it be? Could it be that there's a chance for redemption yet? Praise Him, could it really be?"

Convinced that his companion was well in body, but concerned suddenly for the state of his mind, Albert grabbed Malarkey by the shoulders and shook him, hard.

"Malarkey!" he cried, and louder, "Malarkey!"

With a start, Malarkey's eyes focused and then rose to meet Albert's. They stared at each other for long seconds, before the bird looked over at Albert's sword. It lay half submerged in the muck of the blight, covered in blood in the sickly grass.

"Wipe your sword, lad, it'll rust," he said, and turned away.

He would say no more.

Chapter Ten

Albert and Malarkey sat in silence as their heartbeats and breathing returned to normal. Slowly, gingerly, they each began to run their hands down their body, patting gently and trying to determine the extent of their injuries. Amazingly, they had escaped relatively unscathed; Albert had a gash across his forehead and some ribs that felt tender when he took a deep breath. Malarkey's sword arm was bruised and the creature's cruel spines had neatly sliced the webbing between two of his toes. Malarkey wiggled them, experimentally, wincing as the pain shot up his foot.

"Still, it will bear weight," he murmured. Their ability to continue determined, the duo rose to their feet, moving with the wincing care of very old men, and began to collect their belongings. Item by item, they carried their stores to the outer boundary of the blight, far from the remains of the Chordra, and laid the lot in a pile on the grass. Their water skins and weapons were, blessedly, undamaged, though their sleeping rolls and spare set of clothing, like the clothing they wore, were ripped and torn but still better than nothing. Albert's baseball, though scuffed, had survived, as had the framed photograph of a lovely young penguin that Malarkey had hidden in his knapsack. The fish caught earlier had been trodden to mush, and most of the hardtack rolls that Malarkey had brought with were no more than just so much powdery dust. It was impossible not to be disheartened by the depletion of their supplies, and Albert and Malarkey stared silently.

Finally, Albert spoke. "What do we do now?" he croaked, his throat sore with the combination of disuse and his cries from earlier. Malarkey did not answer for a long while, so long that Albert thought for a moment that the bird had not heard him.

He was just about to repeat himself when Malarkey replied. "We have enough food left for two days, three if we're careful."

"Do we go back?" Albert asked.

"I think not, young Albert," Malarkey replied. "I think the only thing to do now is move on."

"To where?"

Malarkey sighed and pointed with one flipper to the lonely sea of grass that lay on the horizon. "To the north. To the plains."

"What will we do about food?"

"Trust," said Malarkey, "that the King's land will provide."

The next few days passed in peaceful monotony. Up at dawn, bank the fire, break camp, and spend the day pushing through the waist high grass that still stretched, unbroken, to the horizon. Around the campfire each night

Albert and Malarkey would regale each other with tales from their homes. Albert learned of the great Minotaur city of Yeblerk; a collection of great monoliths made of stone in the shape of a circle, without a single wall inside to divide the buildings. Once upon a time, or the story said, a Minotaur had been imprisoned inside a maze, and the citizens of Yeblerk were determined that it not happen again. He learned about Rohodan, the great shark that legend said lived in the deepest part of the Cerulean Sea. Rohodan could eat an entire schooner in a single bite, and harpoons sprung from his back like the quills of a porcupine, but he felt not one. Most of all about the King and His son, the Prince. Once, a plague had struck the trolls that lived deep inside some caves north of the Castle. It was a fearsome sickness, rotting them while still alive. Those who did not die instantly tottered about on withering legs, supporting themselves on canes and staves with arms that fared no better. They could not grow or hunt for food and as a result even those not affected were little more than

skeletons with bowl-shaped protruding bellies. They implored the cities, asking for food, for medicine, but their cries fell on ears deafened by fear. No one would approach, so terrified were they that they would fall ill next, and so they were shunned by all. All that is, except the Prince. One day, the Prince strode into the colony of caves, unguarded and unafraid. One by one, he laid his hands on the beleaguered trolls and they watched in wonder as their bones knit together, their skin healed. By the end of the day, the plague had disappeared. Another time, a pack of wolves, fierce and the size of small horses had besieged a village. They ripped the inhabitants limb from limb, carried the children away only to turn them into wolves themselves. Finally, the villagers had no choice but to flee, leaving the only home that they had even known. The wolves pursued, picking off the slowest of the refugees, pushing them beyond all endurance. Finally, the beleaguered villagers reached a great river. Seeing how fast and furiously the river flowed they wept, pounding at their chests and crying out to the King for mercy. Suddenly, the water swelled until it seemed higher than a mountain and the riverbed was dry save for small puddles and flopping fish. There was pandemonium; with a wall of water in front of them and the wolves right behind. What could be in store but certain death? Then, the wave crashed behind them, drowning the wolves and clearing a path for the villagers to cross.

"Everyone knows it was the King," Malarkey said, "even though no one saw Him."

"I'm not sure how I feel about the King," Albert said, after he heard this tale. "He sounds scary." Malarkey stared into the distance, considering.

"I suppose He is," he said at length, "but mostly only if you're a wolf."

Malarkey, for his part, heard of great buildings that pierced the sky. "You have that many castles?" he squawked in wonder.

Albert shook his head.

"No, they weren't even castles," he corrected. "More like marketplaces or lots of houses all stacked up on each other." If the skyscrapers were awesome, then airplanes bordered on disbelief.

"Flying carriages?" the bird asked again and again. "Flying *horseless* carriages? What kind of magic is that?"

Albert tried to explain that it wasn't magic at all, but instead things like lift and drag, but as he watched Malarkey's eyes glaze over, much as his often did in particularly boring school lessons, Albert decided to abbreviate his lesson and moved on to the battle of the Alamo, something much closer to Malarkey's liking.

One day, around noon, Albert thought that he saw something on the horizon. However, the sun was high and the air was hot, causing visions of puddles up ahead that resolved themselves to nothing but more grass, and making the air itself seem to quiver. And so Albert said nothing, took a sip of water from his waterskin that was barely enough to coat his parched tongue, and walked on. An hour later by the sun he looked again. This time there could be no doubt, there was definitely something up ahead. It was a wall, made of large slabs of prairie earth baked to a golden brown. A dozen or more birds circled overhead. "Vultures," Albert thought to himself with a shudder. Suddenly, one of the birds yelled to another. "Higher, son. You must go higher!" In response, another of the creatures launched itself upward. Higher and higher in the sky it went, and just as it reached its apex, enormous wings unfurled. One after another the others followed, until all of the vultures, obviously not vultures at all, were but pinpoints in the sky, moving gracefully in infinity signs and loop the loops.

"Malarkey, look!" Albert exclaimed in delight. The bird raised his head. He had been plodding along, uncomplaining, and so Albert didn't realize until that moment how miserable his friend was. The bird's beak was dry and powdery, and tufts of feathers were starting to come loose around his shoulders.

"Are you all right?" Albert spurt.

"It's the heat," Malarkey replied. "The sun, mostly. I'll be just fine once there's some trees or a roof overhead for a bit."

"Should we hurry up there?" Albert asked, pointing at the wall on the horizon. Malarkey stopped, rubbing one flipper over his eyes.

"By the King" he muttered, "Plainsmen. No, lad, we will go around," and he took a sharp turn to the right. Albert did not follow.

"But they will have food there," he cried. "Water. A place where you can rest." Malarkey nodded.

"Indeed they would, but those things are for them, not for us." "I don't understand," Albert cried in dismay.

Malarkey sighed. "Let us set up our tents, then," he said, "I'm about done in. And after a rest, I'll tell you of one of the great tragedies of Gwytthenia."

They fell, then, into a soggy, twitching sleep, rolling and slapping as the flies sampled their sweat and found it tasty. Two hours later they roused themselves, crumpled and sore and less refreshed then when they began. They stretched and sipped at water, gnawing on the sweet stems of the prairie grass. "So, what happened?" Albert asked.

Malarkey breathed deeply. "What happens all too often when cultures collide? Fear. Hate. The Plainsmen, which I should tell you is not their word for themselves, used to roam all over Gwytthenia. They followed the herds, or the seasons, or even just their whims. People often speak of them as simple, but that's not true. They were, are, as complex as anyone," he laughed ruefully. "More complex than some. What they were was ... unencumbered, I guess. The machinations of the King and the Kingdom didn't concern them much. How could they? They most likely weren't there when the decrees were signed, and wouldn't be there for long after. What concern are taxes for those who sustain themselves? Or territory for those who have none? It was inevitable, really."

"What?" Albert asked, leaning forward, "What was?"

"War," Malarkey replied. "The city expanded, as cities do, the villages sprawled. What happened next has been debated for centuries. Some say the Plainsmen attacked first, others say it was the villagers. In any case, at the end of the day there were those from both sides who lay dead. However, the Plainsmen were more experienced, they had lived by their wits and their skill since time out of mind and because they killed easier they were determined to be a threat. And, as any threat, they had to be pushed away. So, the soldiers came and pushed them. They pushed them farther and farther until suddenly the only places they were allowed to roam free was those granted to them." The bird chuckled scornfully. "Granted to them, I tell ye, when that and more was there's to begin with."

"Where was the King during all of this?" Albert asked. Malarkey shrugged.

"Ranging to take care of threats elsewhere. Hearing petitions. Running a Kingdom. He tried to step in. He wrote decrees, even came down to stand in the fray. The villagers were sweet as pie, then, agreed to everything he said, and then when he left they went right back to killing and shoving. Some even said they were fighting in the name of the King. Raised near 'bout an army. Of course, the King wouldn't do such a thing. He punished them, sent them to gaol, but by then the damage was already done."

"So what would happen if we got too close?" Albert asked. "Would they kill us? We weren't even alive then!" Malarkey shook his head.

"No, lad, haven't you been listening? They aren't looking to kill. They aren't violent, bloodthirsty. There are those in this land who are, don't mistake me, but the Plainsmen aren't of that lot. It's a little thing, showing respect, but at this point it's all we can do. And so we shall." Albert nodded sadly, looking at the wall in the distance and hoping to see more marvelous acrobatics. The light was fading fast, though, and the walled village was quiet. Albert was still looking over his shoulder as they left in the morning, his heart filled with a pain that he could neither describe nor explain.

Chapter Eleven

The land was kind the next day. It was rare that Albert and Malarkey went more than a mile without finding a spring by which they could rest, and cool their sunburned faces with splashes of deliciously cool water. Malarkey found some curiously meaty ground berries, dense and savory, and when roasted over the fire, they made a fine meal indeed. That night, Albert scuffed a rough baseball diamond through the grass, using fieldstones as bases, and they played until the stars appeared overhead, Albert giggling wildly as Malarkey waddled, bobbling back and forth, from one base to another.

However, bad luck has a nasty tendency to strike just when our guards are down and so it was that, when said troubles arrived, they hurt twice as much. So it was that the next morning, as the dew still clung like tiny jewels to the tall grasses, Albert startled a large rattletail sunning off the cool of the night on a rock. Too busy looking at the clouds in the sky, one looked like a rabbit, another like a puffy dragon, Albert didn't see the beast until he'd nearly trodden on it. The snake responded as snakes do when their basking is interrupted by nearly being crushed, and struck. With a deftness that would have been impossible just a month before, Albert leapt back as soon as he heard the raspy match strike of scales on rock, and as a result he was spared anything beyond a scare. The snake, no longer threatened, seemed content to let bygones be bygones and so the two parted as amicably as one cold hope for. As well as it ended, and truly one could hardly ask for a better ending, the mishap seemed a portent of the day to come. Albert and Malarkey walked for the greatest expanse of the day without finding a spring. When Albert finally saw a change in the shade of the grass, generally a signal that water was nearby, he sprinted over. The spring was foul with the ick, filled with fetid water and surrounded by sickly looking grass. He fell to his knees, his face in his hands.

Malarkey came up to him and patted him awkwardly on the shoulder. "Best keep going, lad. We will find another before too long."

Malarkey was both correct and incorrect. They did, in fact, find another spring. Three more, in fact which all shared the same unfortunate fate as the first. Just as night began to fall they did find some water, little more than a mud puddle. It was murky, and warm, but drinkable, and they filled their water skins reluctantly at best. The next day was much the same, and so was the day after. The only break in the monotony was unfortunate, as Malarkey found the burrow of a small creature by falling partway into it. His leg twisted as he fell, and Albert had to help him up. The bird continued gamely on, but his wobbling walk was exacerbated and though he claimed not to feel any discomfort, Albert could tell he was in pain. Knowing the noble bird would not stop on his own account, Albert claimed a headache and they made camp early. Just before the sun rose the next day, Albert rose and snuck out of camp. He hoped to find water and be back before Malarkey awoke.

    It became clear, after a mile, that Albert was not going to have such luck, but nevertheless he was enjoying himself. The air was still cool, and the grass made a pleasant "wooshing" sound as he stomped through, scattering bits of dew here and there. At one point, Albert found a stick. He had no idea from whence it came, there not being a tree anywhere nearby, and Albert soon became so enamored with using the stick to chop the furry heads off of the grasses that he completely forgot about looking for water. "Ha!" he yelled, swinging the stick, and a dozen or so heads cartwheeled through the air. "Ha!" he yelled again. "Take that, you villians!" Up hills and down he went, towards every point of the compass, while the sun crested it's zenith and started down again. Albert looked for water, kind of, swinging the stick every now and again for good measure.

    "Are you lame or wounded?" the voice, breathless with exasperation, rang out across the plains. Albert whirled around, his hand at the hilt of his sword. Ten yards behind him stood a girl approximately his age. At least, she was a biped with two humanlooking eyes and one human-looking mouth and she was speaking English.

That was closer to human than anyone Albert had met thus far. She was short and stocky with thick black hair braided back from a high, clear brow. A more observant creature may have noticed that she was not entirely human and an even more observant soul would have noticed that her face was screwed, not against the sun, but rather in consternation. Albert, being overjoyed at the prospect of another human and being, beyond that, a perfectly normal eleven year-old was not exceptionally observant. At home, shoes proved especially elusive.

Here, in a strange land and confronted by a girl, of all things, powers of observation evaded him entirely, which may perhaps explain why he grinned hugely and said, "No, I'm Albert," by way of reply.

The girl huffed a bit. "All right, *Albert*, are you lame or wounded?" As he did not reply but instead just stood, his smile beginning to look increasingly awkward, she elaborated. "What is wrong with your legs?" she asked slowly and loudly, as though she were speaking to someone who was very far away or, perhaps, did not speak her language very well.

Albert startled and looked down. He had assumed, until that very moment, that had something happened to his legs he would be the first to know. But then, as his mother was prone to say, stranger things had happened. So, he bent over, patting first one leg and then the other, carefully, from thigh to ankle "Nothing," he reported cheerfully. "What's your name?"

The girl drew herself proudly to her full height of perhaps four-and-a-half feet. "My name is Ahoka of the Plainspeople," she said imperiously, "and you – *you*" she flopped her paw-like hands down at her side, "You're ruining everything" and with that she threw herself onto her bottom in the grass and buried her face in her hands.

Albert, like many people encountering the unexpected rage of another, deserved or not, stood perplexed, wondering where on earth he had gone wrong. His first instinct, sad to say, was to deny everything. He wanted to stomp his foot and yell things like "I haven't done *anything*," and "It's not *my* fault," even though he didn't know what everything it was that she believed he'd ruined. But instead, he put one foot in front of the other until he found himself next to the weeping girl. It was only at that moment that he noticed that, girl she may be, but that was certainly not all. Her arms and legs were covered in a light fur, tan like the grass, and two wings sprouted from her shoulder blades. She was, quite simply, amazing. "Why, you're incredible!" he exclaimed, unplanned, and then blushed furiously.

Ahoka looked up and smiled just the tiniest bit. "Thank you," she said, wiping her face with her arm, "but I sure don't feel incredible right now. Not at all."

Albert sat beside her, taking a brief swig from his water skin. It was barely enough to wet his mouth, but as the skin was becoming alarmingly light, it would have to do. "Are you lost?" he asked her gently. It was the only thing he could think of that could cause such distress.

She raised her head again and scoffed. "Lost? A Plainsperson is never lost."

"Then what's wrong?"

Ahoka's eyes flashed, and Albert scooted back a bit. "Today was supposed to be easy," she fumed. "There are four tasks I have to complete to be considered a full member of the tribe. The first is to build my own home. I did that. It even stood up the first try! Almost everyone takes two tries, or even more, but I did it. Then, I had to gather plants for medicine. That was harder because, well, my grandma says I have busy eyes." She scratched absently at an insect bite on her leg, and Albert saw that her arms ended in paws instead of the hands he expected. Even sheathed, the claws were fearsome. He swallowed with great effort and fought the urge to scoot away once more.

She continued, "But I did that too. Then we have to spend the night by ourselves blindfolded. I didn't even cry. They say everyone cries, but I didn't. Last, we have the Feed the Feast."

"What is feeding the feast?" Albert asked. He plucked a piece of grass and pinched it between his thumbs and then blew, trying to make it whistle. He had been trying to master that trick for years with no success, nor was it any different that time. Ahoka glared at him.

Albert put the blade of grass down.

"Feeding the Feast is when you go out hunting by yourself. Whatever you bring back is what is cooked to celebrate your entrance into the tribe."

"So what happens if you don't bring enough?" Albert asked. "I mean, sometimes all mom makes for dinner is mac and cheese or cold raviolis from the can, but it's still dinner."

Ahoka mouthed the unfamiliar words trying to parse what he'd said. Albert watched her try "ravioli" tree times before she gave up. Still, she seemed to glean his meaning. "One who cannot feed the tribe has no place in it," she said simply. "I bragged that I would have the biggest feast ever. I didn't mean it. The purple buffalo have moved east and there's nothing as big as those. I still thought that it would be easy, though. I've been hunting with my brothers since I was small. It was supposed to be easy, but now the day is almost done and I have nothing and it's all your fault."

The last three words snapped out like the crack of a whip and Albert flinched. "How is it my fault?" he exclaimed.

"You're so loud!" Ahoka replied. "You are so loud and you are everywhere. Stomping this way, thumping that way. You've sent all of the game to ground and I'll never get enough in time."

Albert hung his head and slumped his shoulders. "I was just looking for water," he mumbled.

Ahoka leapt to her feet in frustration. "Water! She said, "King above! There's no water here. Do you see signs of water?"

"I don't kn-"

"Do you see green? Do you see plants growing taller than the grass? Do you see soil instead of clay?" Albert shook his head dumbly.

"Then there's no water! Come," she said, stalking off, "I'll take you to it. Maybe we'll find some game there; but you must be quiet."

Albert scrambled to his feet and hurried after her, trying with all of his might to place his feet down gently. He regretted every "ha!" of the day, every beheaded stalk of grass.

"Not like that," Ahoka said, "Watch." And with each step she lifted her foot high above the grass and placed it, gently, toes first. "This is how you quiet-walk. It's called toe-stepping."

Albert copied her, feeling incredibly foolish, but after a couple of steps he realized that it was working. There was hardly a "woosh" at all. Well, less of a "woosh," anyway. Ahoka led them, straight as an arrow, to where a tiny creek wound its way through the plain. When finally it was in sight, lonely except for the chattering and burbles it made talking to itself.

Albert looked at Ahoka, his eyebrows raised, but she shook her head. "Still too loud," she said.

Albert filled his water skin slowly, forlornly, as Ahoka deftly sharpened a stick to a point and went to work in the shallow water, spearing the silver fish that darted to and fro. By the time Albert had finished, she had six plump fish hanging on a string from her belt.

"Is that enough?" Albert asked.

The Plainsperson looked downwards. "Not by far," she said and then raised her eyes to the sun which was hanging far lower. "I'd better go take down my house," she said, and began to walk away.

"You did much better, though," she called back over her shoulder.

Albert chewed on his lip, his brow furrowed. Somehow he had to make it right. He took a step and winced as a twig broke under his feet.

"That's it!" he grinned widely. "Ahoka, wait," he yelled, running after her, "I can help! We can do it together."

She turned slowly and gave him a sad little smile. "Thank you, but I told you, I have to take them alone."

"Well, what do the rules say exactly? Do you have to kill them alone or do you have to be alone the whole time?"

"It doesn't matter; you're still too loud."

"I know," Albert said with a laugh. "I know and that's how I will help!" Ahoka looked at him with one dark eyebrow raised, dubious. "Just trust me," Albert said, "can you do that?"

She shrugged, "I guess you can't make it any worse," she said.

"Okay, right." Albert was too excited to be offended. "Go that way," he motioned over the rise and towards the horizon, "and just wait."

Once Ahoka left, Albert sat very still and counted to one thousand. At least, he was pretty sure it was one thousand. It might have been a little more. Or a little less. He lost count a couple of times. Slowly he rose to his feet and stared in the direction that she had gone, lifting his knees up high and setting his foot down gently, testing the ground before he put any weight on it. He walked a quarter of a mile that way, his heart bounding as the sun slid towards the earth until he felt in his heart, just felt, that it was time. He filled his lungs. "Here goes nothing," he murmured and sprang.

Whatever the opposite of toestepping was, that was what he did. He was loud stepping. Loud running. He screamed. He yelled. He waved his arms back and forth over his head as he crashed, zigzagging though the grass. At first there was nothing, and Albert's spirits sank. Then, with a fierce thrumming three birds, fat, squatty and brown, burst from the grass and into the air, squawking their indignation. Albert didn't see the Plainsgirl appear. She was just there, her arrows flying.

Albert spun hard to the left and took off again, startling two large rabbits. *ZZZsssnap*! *Zzzsssnnap*! They fell as well. Albert was winded, his side screaming, and still he threw himself back to the right. He nearly tripped over the creatures nestled in the grass before they too decided to bolt. They moved like deer but were striped like tigers, one horn sprouting from the middle of their heads. Three flaps of her wings and Ahoka took the smallest unilope to the ground with her claws, murmuring something in its ear before plunging her dagger into its chest.

Albert stopped. "Is it enough?" he panted, holding his ribs. The girl grinned, smiling fully for the first time.

"If I hurry," she said, and with that she heaved the unilope over her shoulders, and took off across the prairie.

"Good luck," Albert yelled after her.

It was full dark by the time Albert made it back to camp, and for a few terrifying moments he was afraid he'd lost his way. Malarkey had started a campfire, and built it up larger than usual. Albert suspected that was not an accident. Malarkey opened his beak as soon as Albert entered the fire's glow, and from the look in his face it was clear that he was going to fuss. Most likely strenuously. His mother had had that same look, once, when Albert had wandered off at a park, following a small beetle as it trundled through the grass. He'd gotten lost, and had been wandering around crying and snotting when a kindly policeman had found him and taken him to find his mom. The look she'd had, fear and anger and love all rolled into one, had been even more scary than the bit of time he'd spent lost.

Thinking quickly, he tossed one of the full water skins gently to the bird. "I found water," he said. "It took me a while."

Malarkey took a long drink, dipping his beak in the skin's opening. "Clearly," he said, once he'd swallowed. "And did ye no' think you should have told me where you'd gotten to?"

Emboldened by Ahoka, and by his success, Albert raised his chin a bit. "You would have just insisted on going with me, and probably hurt yourself worse. I'm sorry you were worried, but I was okay. I made a friend."

Malarkey raised one eyebrow, making his fringe wiggle. "It was a Plainsperson," Albert said, holding his hands up before Malarkey could interrupt. "She found me, not the other way around. She was nice."

Malarkey stared at him, contemplating. "All right, then," he said at last, and took another drink of water.

Albert's last thought, before he fell asleep, was of Ahoka and whether or not she'd gotten back in time. He really hoped she had. The next morning, Albert rolled over and bumped up against something hard in the grass beside him. He opened his eyes, and found a small clay pot, filled with a thick, meaty stew. A bracelet made of beads and leather was looped around the lid.

Albert smiled as he tied the bracelet on. "Look, Malarkey," he said, "I got us some breakfast!"

Chapter Twelve

For two days, they travelled. On the third, they trudged. Their heads ached from squinting against the sun, and their tummies ached for lack of drink. Ahoka's stew was but a pleasant memory. They drank the last of their water in the early morning, and by noon Malarkey called them to a panting halt.

"Let's grab a rest, boy," he said. "It's too hot and we can't spare the sweat. We'll start out again once the sun's gone down."

"What happens then?" Albert asked, desperately hoping for some strange night magic, hitherto unknown to him.

"Hopefully we'll find water," Malarkey said simply. "And if we don't, I'd rather cover the miles by the light of the moon than by that of the sun." Albert nodded, disappointed, heaving a sigh that only filled his lungs with the thick muggy air and making himself feel worse.

It was one of the longest nights Albert had ever known. His eyes were grainy, and it hurt to blink. His whole body, in fact, was sore and weary, and by midnight he could barely put one foot in front of the other. Until that night, Albert had not known how completely and devastatingly black a Gwytthenian night could be without the comforting glow of a campfire. They passed the night in miserable silence, staggering through the grass. Albert tripped over a rock once, stubbing his toe quite badly. The trickle of blood was, in its own way, more irritating than the wound itself, and he kept scuffing his feet to wipe the crimson ooze away, then walking double-time to catch up with his friend. Sometime after midnight they staggered into some unseen brambles and spent ten minutes trying to extricate themselves without injury, and failing. Dawn came slowly, creeping up from the eastern horizon as the air turned from black to grey. Full light had not quite arrived when Albert, more asleep than awake, walked into something hard and unyielding. A small "ouf" from the vicinity of Albert's waist let him know that Malarkey had had a similar encounter. Groggily, Albert rubbed his eyes and shook his head and slowly the object came into focus. It was a fence. The fence reached as high as Albert's chest and wound through the field like a giant black snake, as far as the eye could see.

"What does this mean?" Albert asked. His throat was scratchy and it hurt to speak. When Malarkey replied, his usual caw was little more than a croak.

"It means, lad, that we've reached the outer edges of the great ranches that lie within these plains."

"That's great!" Albert replied. "Surely the rancher would give us some food and water," and he started to scramble between the slats of the fence.

Malarkey spoke quickly. "Easy up, lad, give me a moment to think."

"What's there to think about? I'm hungry."

"Ranchers are hard folks; they have to be. The land is hard, water can be scarce, and thieves certainly aren't. When health and safety of a few hundred cattle or horses are all that are standing between your family and starvation, you tend to be a bit wary of strangers."

"A bit wary, what does that mean?"

"It means they're likely to loose an arrow first and ask questions after."

"Well," Albert scratched absently at an insect bite on his leg. "What are our options then?"

"If we cross on to the land there's a chance we won't make it…"

"And?"

"And if we don't, we certainly won't make it."

Albert smiled wryly and began to walk across the field. He called back over his shoulder to the penguin lingering behind the fence. "What are you waiting for?"

The duo took a minute to suck on the dew that had collected on the tall reeds, and while neither got quite enough, even a little is a lot when it's sitting next to nothing. Thus refreshed, they collapsed into a sweaty, twitching sleep filled with dreams of the angry rancher that may or may not lie ahead. Malarkey woke first, and looked down at his traveling companion. Albert was sleeping soundly, with his hair stuck in spikes that pointed every which way and in repose he looked younger than ever. Malarkey took pity on the boy, and tarried as long as possible before waking the exhausted child that fate, or the King, or some combination of both had laid in his path. Albert woke in a foul humor, smacking his lips grumpily.

"My teeth are woolly," he said.

"Indeed," said Malarkey. "Even so, we'd best move on."

The day passed without incident, and just as evening fell, the pair came across a small spring that bubbled happily into a small pool. Albert fell immediately to his stomach and stuck his entire head under the water.

"Easy lad, easy," Malarkey warned. "Ye'll only make yourself ill."

Albert paid no mind and was, indeed, immediately and noisily sick. The bird, having only taken small sips, took himself to the task of finding and preparing a small meal while Albert recovered. It was an early night and a much-needed rest for the weary travelers, and they pushed through the grass with renewed vigor the next morning. By early afternoon, they could see vague shapes moving in the distance. As they approached the herd, Albert saw the sun glinting off of something golden. The metallic shimmer seemed to be floating above the heard of, well, whatever it was that was out there. Albert strode forward, his brow furrowed, not watching at all where he was going and didn't even stop when he stomped on Malarkey's foot, causing the bird to let out a cry more weary than indignant. Twentyfive yards closer, fifty, and Albert let out a cry of delight.

"Carousel horses!" He said, "Malarkey, those are carousel horses, and they're *alive*!" One of the horses heard him and gave a whinny of alarm. Soon, the whole herd was thundering away from the fence.

"Down! Quiet!" Malarkey hissed, grabbing at Albert's arm. Albert and Malarkey dropped below the waving tops of the grass and began to crawl. It was tough going, and Malarkey got stuck several times. Once a snake slithered dryly over Albert's arms, and he bit his tongue hard to keep from screaming. The paddock ahead was just visible through the grass when suddenly the air was pierced with a throaty scream.

"YEEEEEEEEEEE-HAAAW," the voice cried. "Imposters! Git 'em! GO GET THEY-UM!" Before Albert could turn his head towards the sound, he found himself jerked into the air by a rope that had seemingly wound itself around his heels. A few short seconds later his arms and legs were bound together and held straight up in the air. Malarkey was similarly trussed on Albert's right, and out of his line of sight, he could hear his captor fussing. "I caught me some durn rustlers," the husky voice muttered, "gol-durn rustlers right here on my land." A gigantic hat cast an equally large shadow across Albert's face, and as his eyes focused he saw the wrinkled wizened face below.

Suddenly the scowling face relaxed into a smile. "Well I'll be a kitten's mitten, it's a real live human.

Fifteen minutes later, Albert and Malarkey, unbound and having had long and luxurious drinks and scrubs at the cistern outside the great house's door, were seated at the long, low, scrubbed wood tables in the dwarf's dining room. The gentleman himself, he had introduced himself as Tex Colander, was busily working at the stovetop. Tex was tiny, he barely came up to, well, Albert thought it would be his bellybutton, but he wasn't quite sure. The hat, comically large and perpetually falling around Tex's ears, added at least a foot to his height and perhaps more. The dwarf hadn't said much, at least not to the travelers directly, though he kept muttering excitedly to himself and throwing furtive, almost disbelieving glances over his shoulder. He was acting, in fact, much as you and I would if a member of the British Royal family showed up at the door and requested tea.

Soon, but not before the wonderful aroma had begun to make both Albert and Malarkey drool, Tex laid before them what he called "some proper vittles." There were mountains of beans, an unidentifiable but delicious meat smothered in gravy, and a type of bread that was both like and unlike the cornbread of our world, made from the grain that covered the plains. Albert ate a great many slices of the latter, smeared with butter and thick Gwytthenian honey. Nobody spoke while they ate, Albert and Malarkey because of hunger and Tex out of a ranch hand's many years of habit. When finally they were finished, Tex leaned back in his chair, released a long reverberating belch, and produced a pipe from the pack he wore at his waist. Malarkey joined him with remarkably little persuasion and soon they were both puffing out great clouds of sweet smelling smoke.

"So tell me, young'un," he asked Albert at last. "Does the good King Elvis still reign supreme over your United States?"

Albert was flabbergasted. "Um, no. He … died quite a while ago."

Tex looked devastated and reached out to pat Albert's shoulder gently. "It's always a shame when a country loses its King. Why, I'll never forget the great musical speech I saw your King give. Dressed all in jewels he was, with thousands and thousands of compadres. He sang of the tenderness and truth of hearts and how we should all try to avoid cruelty at all costs. It's moved me, boy, and t'was as purty, as purty as a sunset over the Rockies." Here the little dwarf actually burst into large noisy tears, and produced a red bandana nearly as large as himself. He mopped at his eyes for a bit, then blew his nose noisily.

Albert choked back laughter. "Thank you, sir," he said, "but its okay. Elvis was just a singer. They called him "The King" but he wasn't really. We don't even *have* kings in the United States."

"No, young'un, I surely do appreciate you tryin' to make me feel better, but there's no use lyin'. I consider myself to be a bit of an expert on your land, spent a racoon's age there way back in, oh, years ago now and t'was only in little bits at a time. Still, I tell you that man was the King!" And again he buried his face in his bandana. Malarkey, not exactly fond of emotion of any sort, was looking disgusted, and Albert, very uncomfortable, grasped for anything that could distract the small rancher.

"Well, you still have your King," he said, slightly desperately.

"We do, we do at that," the rancher nodded vigorously. "Yup, and there's no one like Him. Still, though, it was nice to be in a place where there was a King you could see."

"A King you can see? Can't you see yours?"

'Well, not 'zactly. Y'see, He ain't a ghost or invisible or nothing like that, it's just that, well, He pretty much stays in His castle nowadays. If anyone is out and about it's the Prince and He don't come round here much."

"W-what else did you do in my ... Kingdom?" Albert stammered. Tex's face, hangdog and tearstained, split in a wide grin.

"Movies," he yelled. "Ah Pure-D loved goin' to one a them moving picture show." Albert grinned.

"I like going to the movies too! Cartoons and superheroes and action," he mimed holding a rifle, "eh-eh-eh-eh Blammo!" he said.

"I dunno about alla them," Tex replied. "I allus watched Westerns. In fact, that's how I picked mah name. Never much cared fer the one mah mamma gave me. It's hard to be a rough and tumble rancher when yer name is, he lowered his voice and whispered, "Dimbell," but Tex, that's a fine name. Real fine."

"And popcorn," Albert reminisced.

"Um-*um*," agreed Tex. "Ah allus got me a big ol' tub of that poppin' corn. Why this one time ..."

Tex and Albert spent the next hour talking about their favorite movies while tall shadows grew on the walls and Malarkey looked, bemused, from one to the other.

"And after," Tex continued, "I'd allus go pay mah respects at the temple."

"Temple?" Albert was mystified.

"Shore! You know the temple, it's got this big golden castle outside and if you give a title to the priests, the gods would bless you with vittles."

"You mean ... VonBurger?" Albert asked.

"Yee-haw! That was it! The shrine of VonBurger."

"But that's not ...who told you it was a shrine?" It seemed like the kind of jokes that some of the boys in Albert's class would like to play on someone, and his face flushed in secondhand embarrassment for his new friend.

"No one told, me boy!" Tex replied. "They didn't need to. I knows a temple when I sees one."

Albert, rather prudently, decided to let it go. "When was the last time you were in my kingdom?"

Tex kicked his worn and oversized boots up on the table and lit his pipe, which sent multicolored puffs of sweet-smelling smoke up towards the celling. "It's been a long time that's for sure. Seems like nobody hardly wants carousel horse's nummore." His lips and eyebrows turned downwards. "But I ain't ever knowed nothin else so I just keep on."

Suddenly, Albert sat straight up, his feet hitting the wooden floor with a thump. His eyes were wide and shining. "But you know a way there!" he shouted.

"A-yuh," Tex said. "The King placed a portal nearby. Hid it good. You's could only go through with permission. 'Course I allus got permission." Tex looked at them slyly. "When He found out how much I liked it there, He's the one who told me I could tarry a bit." "You could take me home!" Albert hadn't heard much past "portal." "Oh Tex, please, I promise it won't take long," he begged.

Malarkey held up a flipper. "Nay, Lad," he said, "If you're here, there's a reason for it. Ye must go the King and find out what it is."

"You don't know that," Albert snapped. "You don't know if there's a reason any more than I do. It could have been an accident or a mistake or…"

"Now fellas," Tex interjected, his voice mild. "Aint no use in getting' all riled up. I cain't do it nohow. The King, He were mighty particular about who went back and forth and I ain't looking to break His rules. Why, He could shut down the portal iff'n I did something like that. Even if

He didnt, there ain't no way I could take a young pup like you out there now. Things are gettin' dangerous round here. Strange lights in the sky. Strange critters wanderin' round. I get a vagabond here every now and again and the stories they tell, hoo-eee they'd make your hair stand up clear on end. Nope. I figure I'm stayin' right here where it's safe, and tendin' to my hosses." He yawned and stretched luxuriously. "Speaking of which, ah guess it's time to turn in. Ah'll see y'all bright n' early."

Malarkey and Albert bedded down in a bunkroom that, in more prosperous times, must have held twenty workers or more. After weeks in forests and fields it felt as luxurious as a castle. Something about the place seemed odd, though. Not unpleasant, just different, and it niggled at the back of Albert's brain like a fishhook. As he snuggled down into the feather tick and pulled a worn quilt, a lone star pattern made of soft pastels, over himself, it finally hit him. The ranch was built for dwarves. Thus, with everything in miniature, it fit Albert perfectly. He had grown accustomed to living in an adultsized world but, once he discovered the difference, he found that he enjoyed it immensely. Mystery solved, he yawned and rolled over. He felt like he could have happily slept for a week. "Good night,' he murmured to Malarkey, but the bird was already asleep.

Chapter Thirteen

Tex woke the duo before the sun had even cracked the horizon. He was almost insufferably chipper. Albert's eyes, when he saw the breakfast spread laid before him, grew as large and round as the sunny-side-up eggs that snuggled themselves up between sausages and berry-speckled muffins. He ate until he was stuffed, his stomach distended, and thought to himself that it may well be a week before he was hungry again. He was surprised, however, to find said stomach rumbling loudly by the time that the sun stood straight overhead. Hay season was at its epoch, and Tex had sent Albert to exercise the horses while he and Malarkey headed for the fields. "Ah reckon they feel a little neglected-like, and when carousels get restless they can tear things up worsen a twister."

Albert could see the dwarf and penguin in the distance, standing atop a machine that seemed entirely composed of cogs, gears, and rust, yanking up and down on a lever. The machine trundled through the hay, laying a wide path littered with tidy bundles behind it. Albert didn't have much time to watch their progress, however, he had his own hands gleefully full. The horses were , in fact, quite restless, and Albert took one at a time to the small exercise pen where he attached them to a lead and ran them in circles just as the old rancher had instructed. It was a comical and wondrous sight, with their poles glistening in the sun and their poles moving up and down as they ran. When the ponies were well-winded and Albert was dizzy he would hitch them to a post and give them a pail of cool water. Then he would curry them, brushing the dirt and dust out of their coats, untangling their manes, and shining their tall brass poles. He talked to them as he worked, and stroked their velvety noses. He was amazed to discover that they each had their own distinct personalities. The older horses were, as a rule, more sedate, regal. One, a truly ancient pinto named Glimmer, was outright crotchety. She tried to nip Albert repeatedly, and even refused the golden applelike bits of fruit that the others devoured. In contrast the younger horses, not quite colts but not far from it, were jovial. They cavorted in the air and nudged their jeweled heads against Albert's arms, demanding more scratches. They seemed more like cats than horses. Albert's favorite by far was one of the youngsters. Sapphire was written in golden script on his saddle. He was a glistening silver with deep midnight eyes and a flowing mane. He followed Albert like a puppy, nickering affectionately. By the time Albert had exercised the whole herd the sky had turned the odd golden hue that, while not quite sunset, signaled that the end of the day was upon him. Wiping the sweat from his brow, Albert wandered out to the hayfield. A third of the field had been baled by that point, and Albert spelled a grateful

Malarkey at the end of the last row. That evening passed much as the one before, with the three companions sharing tales of their adventures. Albert came to have a great deal of affection for the grizzled old dwarf. His memories of Earth were hugely romanticized and hilariously off the mark, but even so he was, somehow, a bit of home. And Malarkey, Albert discovered to his delight, wasn't nearly as somber and cranky as he had been ever since Albert had met him. Even as some of the tales left Albert slapping the table and wiping tears of mirth from his eyes, he couldn't help but wonder what had changed the bird so drastically.

The next two days passed much the same as the first; there was just so much work to be done. At dinner the second night, after they'd washed the dust off of their faces, Albert asked a question that had been worrying at him all day. "Tex? Why are you here all alone?" Malarkey started to hush Albert, but the rancher held up one hand. "It's all right, Malarkey. Mah mama allus said t'was better to ask."

Tex picked at a dried up piece of bean that had been missed by the washrag and stuck to the table. "Part of it's like I told ya before, there ain't many who wants carousel hosses nummore. Your world has changed, lad, and not for the better iff'n you ask me. But it's not just that. Our world has changed, too. It just got to where I couldn't hardly trust no one anymore. Had one feller stop by, nice enough looking lad, but after helping me dig a well one day he came back in and just went crazy, his eyes went all goldybrown and he started knocking stuff over. If it hadn't been for my lasso I'da been in a whole heap of trouble. Another group a folks came in all beat to tarnation. Said some scaly thing with big claws and lotsa heads had set on them on the way here."

Albert sat straight up and mouthed "Chordra" to Malarkey, who nodded back. The dwarf, lost in thought, didn't notice. "I patched 'em up, told them they could stay, but they were purty eager to get on their way. I couldn't blame em." Tex sighed. "Times are a changin' boy. So, I take on a bit of help in the busy seasons, foaling, autumn storms and the like. Mostly, though, I take care of my own." When he looked up, his eyes were wet. "Still, it's nice to have you all here. A man can get a might lonesome all on his own." Albert found himself wishing wistfully that he could stay there at the ranch permanently. Malarkey, though, was growing restless. Albert could see him glancing periodically towards the horizon and he knew that their time together was growing short.

"One more day, Lad," Malarkey whispered one night as they lay, sore but content, in their bunks. "One more then we need to be on our way.

"All right," said Albert reluctantly.

*   *   *

The next morning, though, dawned gloomily. Huge, pendulous clouds hung on the horizon, blocking the sun. When Tex came to rouse them from bed his voice was high-pitched with urgency.

"Up and at em boys," he caterwauled, "we gots to move."

"What is it?" Albert asked, hurriedly putting on his shoes.

"It's the autumn storms! They're more than a might early, though! I ain't never seen 'em this soon. They're fierce, though. Ah've seen them throw a giant like it weren't no thing. Let's go!"

There was no breakfast, just scalding hot cups of some grassy tea that they slurped as they rushed out of the door.

The horses were frantic, whinnying and charging around their pens. The younger ones were compliant enough, heading for the bans as soon as the corrals were opened. The younger horses, most of them experiencing their first late-summer storms, were another matter entirely. Only Sapphire came when Albert called him, nickering affectionately even though the whites of his eyes showed all the way around his irises .The others lunged and reared, Albert and Tex dove in among them, clipping lead ropes and leading the horses into safety. Malarkey was nothing short of a wonder. Astrid the back of an older bay named "Majestic," he moved in zigzags behind the herd, edging them closer to the runs. Even with the rancher and the two new apprentices working so that sweat poured down their backs and their knuckles turned white, getting the ponies to safety took hours. By then, the clouds were straight overhead. They hung so low that Albert felt that if he jumped he could touch them. Not that he wanted to, those clouds roiled and danced with eldritch light and rumbles of thunder that Albert could feel but not hear.

Slugging down water from their canteens, the trio rushed to hook four of the calmest horses to the hay cart. A soaking rain could mold the hay, leaving the horses hungry come winter. The rows of bales disappeared into the cart with excruciating slowness, though Albert could feel the progress they were making in the muscles of his arms and back. They were on their fourth cart-full when the storm finally broke. One drop of rain, then two. A crack of thunder and then as if given some sort of signal, the sky fell down. Tex and Malarkey unhooked the horses and together they slammed the doors shut on the barn. Somehow, Albert managed to step on the hem of his pajama bottoms, and winced as he heard the fabric tear. He stumbled, and would have fallen if Tex and Malarkey hadn't grabbed his arms. Together, they ran to a house they could no longer see. Though it had been three minutes or less since gravity had overpowered that first raindrop, Albert, Malarkey and Tex left puddles of water standing on the floor as they stood, panting and shivering, just inside the door. Albert could feel streams running between his shoulder blades and see them dripping from the crags of Tex's face.

Only Malarkey was unfazed. He rustled his feathers a time or two with a look that was downright smug. "You two go get warmed up," he said, "I'll have dinner ready."

Tex reached out and took Albert's hand in one of his own and Malarkey's flipper in the other. His throat worked as he swallowed a few times.

"That came on fast. Never in all my years have I seen them come so fast!" Tex said, "Ida never got it done on myself. I'm much obliged to ya."

Albert reached up, tipped an imaginary cowboy hat. "No problem, Pard," he said in his best drawl.

Tex gaped at him, water dripping off of his bulbous nose and mouth hanging open. Then he laughed. Laughed so hard he almost shook the rafters.

Chapter Fourteen

The first night of the great storms passed joyfully, if wearily. Albert implored Tex for a needle and thread, and mended his pajama bottoms with a blanket over his lap, as they sat by the fire.

"Ifn' you don't mind me askin'" Tex said. "What do you call them fancy duds?"

"Pajamas" Albert mumbled around the thread he was wetting.

Tex's mouth moved as he tried out the new word. "Piejarmers" he said at last. "Well if that don't beat all. Back in ma day, people in your world wore somethin' called jeans. But like I said, guess the times are a'changin'"

Albert thought about correcting him, but decided to let it go. Malarkey pulled a chanter from his bag, Tex countered with a ukulele that fit him like a guitar, and Albert pounded on a metal pail, keeping beat the best he could. Together, they played one tune after another. They even tried a rendition of "Don't Be Cruel," though that particular song was most definitely not made for a chanter and after a verse or two Malarkey gave up in disgust.

Tex produced a spiced wine that warmed them and eased their aches and soon they were sharing tales and legends from their peoples. Tex told of how a group of dwarves broke free from the miners during The Great War, and joined sides with the King. They were shunned by the others of course, and chose to forge their way on the prairies. Malarkey spoke of Finnegan the Tall, a penguin who was nearly as large and three times as fierce as a man. Albert, of course, talked about his dad. It was the first time he had been able to speak aloud of him since the man's untimely death. It unlocked a part of his heart that had grown heavy, and as he spoke his tears ran freely. He also discovered, having had adventures himself, that he understood his father better and although he missed him terribly, longed to tell him what he'd been doing in the months since he awoke in a snowdrift. Between the sharing and the bone-deep knowledge that his father would be proud of him, the wound in Albert's heart, gaping since his dad first started to get sick, to disappear for long periods of time, to come back angry and aloof, finally began to heal.

The next day, Tex tried to go out and check on the horses. There was a loud thump and he came crawling back up, holding his bandana to an already swelling nose. "Slat of the barn got me. Tore off and flew all the way to the house. Wind's too durn strong" he said.

"Will the horses be all right?" Albert asked.

Tex looked worriedly outside the window. "I guess they'll hafta be. The King's Will," he said.

By the next evening, Albert, Malarkey and Tex began to grow restless. They caught each other staring out the window, trying to open the door against the wind, and they grew short-tempered and snappish. The gusts died down a little, but not much.

"Ah reckon tomorrow I'll have to check on the horses no matter what," Tex murmured.

"Tomorrow we may have to head out, rain or not," Malarkey replied. Tex sighed.

"Ah won't tell ya what to do," he said, "but that Feast ain't worth dying over."

"Feast?" Albert was confused.

"I guess I just figgered you boys were headed to the Great Feast. It's about this time 'a year. I don't' go myself, too many folks and I ain't too good at small talk and fancy duds, but most everyone else tries to make it."

Albert looked quizzically at Malarkey.

"The Great Feast, lad. It's a time of great celebration right around harvest time. People come from all over the land and gather near the Castle. The Knights are there, and the White Court. The centaurs and the satyrs and even some Plainspeople. A little bit of everyone."

"Does the King come?" Albert asked.

"I don't know," said Malarkey, "he used to."

"That's great!" Albert said, "I can talk to Him then! That will make things easier!"

But the bird was far away, staring into the distance.

"Easier," Malarkey said, "and harder, too." He sighed.

That night Albert could not sleep. His body had gotten used to hard work and after three days of being housebound he felt effervescent, his legs twitchy. His mind was restless as well, anxious to be on his way, but sad to leave Tex. Afraid they would miss the feast, but nervous about what he may discover. He heard a rustling from the upper bunk and knew that Malarkey was plagued by insomnia just as much as he. The bird spoke, as if reading his mind. "We can still make it, Lad," the bird said, "if we walk fast and the King is willing, we can make it. We will have to leave tomorrow."

Albert listened to the rain pounding on the tin roof. "If the King wills it," he said.

Albert was roused at dawn by a rosy-golden light falling across his face. He slit his eyes, confused, and tried to go back to sleep.

The bunkroom door slammed open with a sound like a rifle shot.

"Yeeee haw!" Tex yelled, tossing his ridiculous hat up to the rafters. "Take a look outside, fellers!" Albert opened his eyes again and gazed out of the window. The clouds were gone. The sky was bathed in sunlight, and at the horizon the pink was already turning to a clear cerulean. Raindrops hung from every surface, reflecting the light into diamonds. Already the trees and grass, pummeled by the rain, were starting to stand again. Albert grinned and stretched, climbing out of bed. He looked at

Malarkey, who nodded. "All right then," he said. "Let's get ready to go."

Albert and Malarkey began to pack their few belongings into their sacks, and while Malarkey was the model of efficiency, a place for everything and everything in its place Albert found himself dithering. He knew they had to leave, could feel the pull of the Harvest Ball and whatever it was that had yanked him unceremoniously out of his world and into this one. Still, he hesitated. It had been nice, the lodge and the meals and the friendship. Even the work. It was good work, and he could see the difference that he made. That was somehow easier to bear than the weariness that came from slogging from one point to another, always on alert, never knowing what would come next. He found himself wishing that he had something from his world that he could give to the rancher as a thank you gift, even as he chided himself for being sentimental. If he were to wish for something, shoes or a toothbrush, a lighter, a flashlight, those would be more useful. He couldn't help it, though. Carefully, he emptied out his pack, ridding himself of the effluvium often accumulated by boys of a certain age. Down at the bottom, he felt something round and hard. Not without some hesitation, he reached in. It was his baseball. Albert lifted the ball to his face, breathing in the scent of horsehair and sweat, of dirt and grass and summer sun. He remembered the day that he'd caught it and how safe he'd felt in his father's arms. Then, he grinned.

Tex was outside. He'd dashed out the door as soon as he saw them start to pack, muttering about the horses. After three days of rain-soaked confinement, there was no doubt that they needed tending. Still, the dwarf took a rather long time to turn the beasts out and the few times Albert peered out at the stockyards he saw the rancher rubbing at his eyes with his overlarge red handkerchief. Tex returned just in time for lunch, muddy and uncharacteristically subdued. The trio sat for one last meal together, despite Malarkey's
frequent glances towards the door. They ate in silence, so quiet that they could hear the scraping of forks on plates.
At last, they could delay no further. Malarkey held out his flipper.

"We are very grateful for everything you've done," he said brusquely. Tex grabbed the bird with both hands and pulled him close. Malarkey squawked with surprised, but then hugged the rancher back, patting him awkwardly.

"Now fellas, I'm the one who owes y'all a debt. I'da never made it through those storms without ya. But, I think I gots something that'll make it worth your while "

"We really have to…"

"You don't need…"

Tex silenced them with his weathered hands. "It won't take but a New York minute and I aint takin' no for an answer. Follow me, boys."

The travelers trailed along behind him as Tex meandered to the paddocks. Albert was pleased to see that the horses looked well. Tex led them to where one of the ponies had been tethered to a post. Albert took in the silver coat, blue mane and gentle face of Sapphire and a small involuntary sound escaped his throat. Tex's voice was gruffer than usual, deliberately nonchalant.

"Ah figure this little fella will help you get to the Fest on time," he said. Albert opened his mouth a couple of times then closed it, trying to force the words past the lump in his throat. They would not come. He settled for hugging the dwarf as hard as he could. Taking a deep breath, he reached into his bag and pulled out the baseball.

"For a long time, this was my most prized possession," he said, "I got this on the greatest day of my life, at least before I came here. I want you to have it." And he handed the beloved ball to the rancher.

"Aw no, I couldn't," Tex began.

Albert pushed it into his hand, smiling tearfully, "Please. It's yours now."

"A gen-u-ine baseball," Tex said in wonder. "I allus wanted one of these. If'n only I had someone to…" He cut himself short. "All right, boy, all right," Tex said. He pulled his handkerchief out of his pocket and blew his nose, a long, sonorous blast that startled one of the more flightier ponies. His eyes were moist. Still hardly believing his luck, Albert climbed into the saddle, grasping the pole for balance, and Malarkey soon scrambled up behind him.

"Goodbye then," Albert said through a crackling voice, gazing down at his friend.

"Happy trails, son," Tex replied. He slapped Sapphire's flanks. "Giddy up."

When Albert turned around, the rancher was still standing at the gate, his hat raised in farewell.

Chapter Fifteen

Once Albert got used to the nauseating ups and downs of Sapphire's gallop, he was amazed at how quickly the ground disappeared beneath them. Soon, he became more confident and was able to let go of the pole with one hand to scratch Sapphire lovingly between his ears. The carousel horse whinnied in appreciation, lifting his velvety muzzle until it pointed directly into the sky so that Albert could reach all of the itches better. Albert pealed laughter.

"Good boy," he said, "That's my good boy," and spent the rest of the day scratching Sapphire here and there, finding out where the horse most liked to be pet. The ears, Albert discovered, were a definite no, and while the cheeks were a yes, Albert nearly fell out of the saddle trying to reach them. The horse genuinely seemed to enjoy neck scratches, deep where the mane joined the skin, but only the spot between the ears gained the whinny of joy and so that's where Albert focused. By the time the sun began to sink towards the horizon, Tex's homestead was well out of sight, and Albert could see ahead a line of something tall and fuzzy that might with a little imagination be trees.

Sunset came too soon, and as they set up camp and Albert curried Sapphire, he couldn't help but miss the comforts that they had enjoyed for the past week. Malarkey was melancholic as well, turning his chanter over and over in his hands but never actually playing. Sapphire, meanwhile, cropped with remarkable unconcern at the grass nearby. They slept soundly, serenaded by the crickets nearby.

By the time that the green, fuzzy things had resolved themselves definitively into trees, the path, no more than a small divot in the grass, had broadened a bit and little patches of dusty earth were visible here and there. A couple of miles later it had broadened yet more and become a proper road. In the distance, Albert could see the rise of a shingled roof and stood tall in the stirrups, holding onto the gleaming pole rising from Sapphire's back for support and, in his excitement, almost toppling an indignant Malarkey onto the ground. "Is that it?" he asked excitedly. "Is that he castle?"

Malarkey, his feathers still both literally and figuratively ruffled scoffed, perhaps more harshly than intended. "Is that what passes for a castle back in your Am-ric-rer-a?" He struggled as he always did with the foreign syllables. "Nay, lad. That's the Dragonhearth Inn, at the heart of the village of Brun. Truth be told, it's nearly all of the village of Brun."

"You never told me about Brun," Albert said, settling himself in the saddle once again.

"Not much to te-watch out!" Malarkey yelled.

Two fox kits had tumbled out of the tall grass, tussling and wresting directly into the path. Albert tugged hard on Sapphires reins and as the pony danced nimbly to the left the father fox pounced, blocking the kits' bodies with his own.

"Ever so sorry about that," the fox quipped, shooing the kits off of the road.

"Did you hear that?" Albert asked Malarkey.

"Hear what?"

"That fox. He talked!"

"Yes?" Malarkey replied, perplexed.

"It's an animal, and it talked!" Albert explained.

"Ye do realize yer telling this to a talking penguin, do ye not?"

Albert chuckled, chagrined. "Yes, but penguins have always talked here."

"So have foxes." Said Malarkey. "The rabbits don't talk. Why not?" Albert asked.

Malarkey shrugged. "Some animal do, some do not. Only the King knows why."

"But if I'm hunting, how do I know what animals I can take?" Albert was getting frustrated. Malarkey was as well.

"Well, if they say 'nae, do no' kill me, then don't. I don't' have a list for ye, lad! What did you do in your land?"

"In my land, we went to the grocery store!" Albert exclaimed. "Besides, in my world, only humans talk."

Malarkey looked up at him for a moment. "Sounds rather dull," he said at last.

Albert chuckled. "I guess it was."

More and more travelers joined the path as they approached the town. They paid Albert, Malarkey, and their steed no mind, though the same could not be said for Albert. He stared wide-eyed at a trio of centaurs, giggled at a score of tiny fairies that flitted by, and shuddered a bit at five cowled and cloaked figures the glided along the path, moving too smoothly to have feet. Malarkey, on the other hand, grew nervous, looking down whenever anyone got close. When Bern, fully visible now as two stone buildings and a number of pavilions that appeared to have been hastily raised in the past few days, was no more than a quarter of a mile away, the bird abruptly ordered Albert to halt. Albert complied, jigging Sapphire to the edge of the track where the pony started cropping contentedly at the sparse bits of green that grew there. The penguin rummaged at length through their provisions, muttering a bit to himself every now and then, and making notes on a small bit of scroll.

"What are you doing?" Albert asked.

"Around festival time, a bit of a market grows up around the Inn. We'll need to do some shopping; just a few bits and bobs."

Albert looked down at his pajamas. The bottoms of them were shredded, far beyond the ability to be mended, and the seat was very nearly indecent. Beside that, flannel jammies were, Albert had learned, nearly useless outside of temperature controlled environments. Sweltering when the weather was warm and woefully inadequate when it was not.

"Could I get some new clothes?" he asked excitedly. It was the first time in his memory that he had been excited to go clothes shopping. Generally, he avoided it whenever possible and had to be bullied and manhandled into an opinion on the times he was forced to go along. Malarkey nodded before adding one more item to the list. He handed the scroll to Albert and reached into his sporran, pulling out a series of long silver pieces, formed to look like sticks complete with bark and little knots here and there.

"These are twigs," he said, "You use them to pay for items. Just hand them over to the merchant and they'll give you your change. Nothing should cost more than half of a twig. Oh! Get me a cloak if ye would, something with a hood. I'll meet you under the tip of the right wing in the Inn when you're done."

"Wait!" Albert exclaimed, "You're not coming with me?" Malarkey looked around, more of those furtive glances that had gotten increasingly common as of late.

"The marketplace is full of- well, anyone could be there and so I'd best not. You'll do all right, lad," he said.

Albert's brow furrowed. "Malarkey," he asked quietly, "are you a criminal?" His voice was high with concern.

The bird said nothing for a long moment, just stared at his webbed feet as they shuffled in the dirt. "I'm someone who is better off not seen" he said, and began picking his way through tall grass.

"You can't be!" Albert yelled after him. "You just can't be a bad guy!"

Malarkey said nothing; just trudged along.

Uncertain and nervous about being alone, Albert did what most people, consciously or subconsciously, would do in such a situation. That is, he did his very best to look like someone who completely and utterly belongs, who had, as it were, not a care in the world. He straightened his back and puffed out his chest. He raised his chin and pursed his lips. Suddenly, he became very aware of both the motion of the carousel horse and of his own nose, which had swam suddenly and rather prominently into his line of sight. It is rather fortunate that he did not encounter anyone else whilst engaged in such a charade, as he looked in that moment equally foreign and ridiculous. As he got closer to the marketplace, close enough the smell the meat roasting, to hear the chatter and laughter, to see the colors and the creatures, the charade fell suddenly away.

Albert giggled, trying to look in a dozen directions at once. One tables, covered with myriad sizes and colors of rocks, was surrounded by large grey creatures with growly voices who were sampling the stones to their vast enjoyment. Another table seemed to have nothing upon it all, though a couple of shoppers had evidently seen something as they were haggling gamely with the crinkled old crone over prices. Four kids ran by, laughing, and chasing a ball that wobbled this way and that, in joyous defiance of the laws of physics. Two giants hailed one another and came together in an enormous hug that would have crushed Albert had he not pulled Sapphire up. Albert clapped with joy. Though Albert didn't know it, he fit in more in his astonishment than he ever had in his haughty nonchalance. The harvest feast with like Christmas, New Year's, a birthday, and a family reunion all taking place at the big Thanksgiving parade and as such, nonchalance was hardly the order of the day. Therefore, eyes wide and mouths staring, Albert passed through largely unnoticed, save for one shrewd and rather unscrupulous shopkeeper. Said shopkeeper was as ugly on the outside as we was within, with a scar running from his forehead and down past his jawline, pulling both the eye and the mouth into a permanent scowl. Festering scabs and bits of hair sprouted like lichen from his scalp. When Albert tried to pay for his purchases, which amounted to no more than a sewing kit and some dried meats and fruits, the shopkeeper made no move to hand him change. Instead, he simply pocketed the whole twig, and leered at Albert as if challenging him to protest. Albert's mouth went dry and his palms grew moist. He opened his mouth to say something, but managed only a strangled croak, which made the merchant's smile even wider. Suddenly, Albert felt a hand on his shoulder. He followed the hand up to a large, shaggy arm and up again to massive shoulders with a giant great axe visible behind them, and still higher to the bovine face and pointed horns of a Minotaur.

"Is there a problem, son?" the Minotaur grumbled. One of the dark, limpid eyes closed slowly in a wink, and Albert could feel the wind rushing into his lungs in relief.

"Nope," he said lightly. "I'm just waiting for my change."

The hand, four thick fingers tipped with more hooves than nails, left his shoulder and splayed on the table and the Minotaur's shadow fell across the recoiling merchant. "Best be getting on with it, then."

"Yes, sir, of course, sir," and the merchant scrambled in his pouch, dropping various odds and ends in his lap in the process. He lay three bits of twig in Albert's hand, then made a shooing motion.

Albert stared at the Minotaur in gratitude, trying to find the words. Somehow, the Minotaur must have heard them, or at least understood, for he smiled a bit, his velvety muzzle wrinkling. "Run along, son," he said. Albert grabbed Sapphire's reins and ran.

The rest of his purchases went far more smoothly; he bought some clothing from a dwarf who conducted the entire exchange speaking around a darning needle he held between his teeth. He bought something sweet that looked like cotton candy but tasted somehow like summer from a long-eared elf; he was even able to find a children's cloak in a rich hunter green that he thought would fit Malarkey nicely.

He was heading to the inn when he saw one last stall. There was no canopy over this one, not even a table. Instead, a thick and coarsely woven blanket was spread on the ground and covered with wares. A large, hulking creature sat in the middle of the blanket. He was fearsome, almost as tall as Albert was, even though the creature was sitting down. He had pointed ears and grey-blue skin and a heavily bearded face. Still, the eyes above the beard were kind and he smiled at Albert. With one square-fingered hand, he sprinkled little crumbs of bread on the ground, much to the delight of the tiny flock of birds that twittered and flitted around his head. The hulking creature was a Firbolg named Winton. If Albert would have known those names he would have giggled. Winton would not have minded; Firbolgs generally didn't. Firbolgs did however, notice much, and when Winton noticed Albert's hesitance to approach the blanket (he had already purchased everything on his list after all) he nodded encouragingly. Albert nodded back and came closer.

The boy's attention had been caught by something shiny, as boys' attentions often are. In this case, it was a length of ribbon among the rickrack that covered the blanket. The ribbon was blue and threaded with bits of gold that twinkled as they gave back the light of the sun. Small navy stones, faceted into teardrops, dangled from each end. Albert could just picture it woven though Sapphire's mane, glittering as they went to seek audience with the King. It would be just the thing.

He bent to pick it up, and held it up to Sapphire. "What do you think, boy, do you like it?" he asked, scratching Sapphire's forelock.

The pony sniffed it and whinnied in what Albert took to be approval. Albert turned back to the shopkeep and as he did he trod upon something that ground metallically under his feet. He moved to straight out whatever he had mussed and pulled out a smallish chainmail hauberk. It was rusted stiff, but intact, and it looked like it would fit him perfectly. Albert let out an involuntary yelp of joy and held the maille to his chest. The clothing he'd bought, patched and faded but infinitely better than pajama pants, he'd selected and purchased with all of the interest of a young person eating vegetables. They were necessary, but not interesting. This, however, this was interesting. He remembered that sometimes, when he had been particularly well-behaved and his dad was in a good mood, Albert would be allowed to try on his dad's body armor. Granted, this was different, but he had no armor, however, nothing that could protect him, and somehow that just seemed like a thing he ought to have.

"How much is it for these two things?" Albert asked the Firbolg. Winton looked at the boy. As I mentioned, Firbolgs notice much and Winton noticed that not only was the boy very excited about the items, but that he was a good boy and had had a rough turn of luck lately. Winton's heart went out to him.

"I guess I'd take half a stick for that ribbon," he drawled slowly, "Sapphires and gold them's are. And the hauberk, oh, I dunno, quarter stick?"

Albert's face fell. Gently, he laid the hauberk down, smoothing the sleeves. After all, he couldn't get another item for himself and nothing at all for his horse. "I'll just take the ribbon then, please," he said, holding out a half a twig.

Winton didn't move to take it. "Now just one minute," the Firbolg said. "I went and forgot. I'd decided that anyone who bought that ribbon, it being special and all, they could pick something else from my shop for free."

Albert's head snapped up, his eyes bright. "Really?" he asked.

"Yup."

The boy eagerly handed over a half of a twig and shook the Firbolg's hand.

"Thank you! Thank you so much!" he said, and dashed off towards the Inn, Sapphire clopping along behind him. Winton smiled.

Chapter Sixteen

With Sapphire safely hitched to the of the many posts out front, Albert stepped through the carved wooden doors of the Dragon Hearth Inn, and any reservations he had about his ability to find Malarkey disappeared. The dragon from whom the public house got its name was immense. Dull gold like burnished bronze, its body and leathery wings, both of which seemed rather tattered and scarred, covered most of the back wall. The tail ran along, or perhaps was, the central beam.

As Albert goggled, a ruddy-faced dwarf lugged, with some difficulty, a large log to the hearth and chucked it in. He reached into his poke and pulled out a golden coin, which he flicked absently. It landed with a small "chink" among other such coins that littered the floor. Suddenly, a jet of fire, all reds and oranges, shot from the dragon's mouth, setting the log ablaze. Albert laughed in delight. He headed to the hearth, weaving his way among the patrons. He saw the Minotaur who had helped him earlier and waved shyly. Once Albert reached the hearth, he looked closely, intently searching for whatever mechanism would put on so impressive of a display. He'd seen pyrotechnics, fire used for spectacle, before. Once, when his dad and mum had taken him to an amusement park, they went to see a stage show. Right at the end, when the good outer space guys had beaten the bad outer space guys, flames had shot up from the stage, taller than a building. But there, he'd seen the valves that had shot the flames. This, this looked so real. He couldn't see a lever or a valve or a button anywhere. He could see the scales, how they got smaller on the creatures face, how some were scarred and damaged. He could even see a tip of a tooth poking out from under the dragon's lip, but no lever.

He pushed his face even closer to the dragon and was growing uncomfortably warm when the dragon winked lazily at him.

"Oh!" Albert exclaimed. "Oh, you're *real*!" The dragon winked again and Albert, guided by some instinct he didn't know he had, bowed.

"That was well done, boy," a voice murmured behind him. Albert turned. "Mordecai doesn't take to just anyone."

Albert tried to reply. He tried to think of something witty or brave, or even coherent, but alas it was all for nothing. Not that he could be blamed, many a person has been struck dumb by a beautiful woman, and the woman who stood before Albert was the loveliest being he had ever seen. She looked like a sculpture, carved by one of the greats, if a sculpture could capture the way her dark eyes sparkled or the caramel of her skin. A painting, then, one of those hanging on the walls of the museum he visited on a field trip. But know, no painting would capture the kindness or strength that you could just sense. And so, being as absolutely normal as he was, Albert grinned and blushed and hoped that was enough.

"Can I help you, lad?" the woman asked, dimples creasing her cheeks. At last, Albert found his voice.

"Ju-just looking for my friend," he stammered, "we were supposed to meet here."

"Good luck finding him in this throng," the woman replied. "If you need help, just call out."

"What's your name?" Albert asked, as she turned to leave.

The woman's eyes widened in surprise and one eyebrow arched slightly. "Why I'm Kochav, and the Dragon Hearth Inn is mine!"

For a brief, heart-pounding moment, Albert thought that he would indeed have to enlist Kochav's assistance, for try as he might he could not find his friend. He didn't want to look like a child, the fact that he was one notwithstanding, and beyond that he knew that Malarkey would be incredibly displeased. So he squinted into the darkest corners, and finally he saw, just barely, the tips of Malarkey's fringe waving above the top of a table. Breathing a sigh of relief, he walked over and flopped onto the bench, stealing glances at Kochav as she moved around the room.

"The cloak, lad! Did you get a cloak?" Malarkey hissed, snapping Albert out of his mezmorization.

"Oh, right," Albert said, and tossed a bundle of cloth across the table. The cloak swirled dramatically, and Albert stifled a giggle.

For a moment it looked like the cloak was dancing all by itself.

Malarkey poked his beak out of the hood and Albert nodded at the proprietress. "Who is she?" Albert asked. "She's lovely."

Malarkey smiled. "Indeed she is, and if the stories are to be believed, nearly as brave as the King, Himself."

"What stories?" Albert asked. "Will you tell them to me?"

Malarkey motioned with his flipper and a barmaid appeared with two mugs of fruity-smelling liquid brimming with cinnamon and cloves. Malarkey took a sip and sighed in satisfaction. "I could, but if I'm right, that eager young buck is about to do that very thing," he said.

Sure enough, a willowy and pale young man with pointed ears was standing on a table by the hearth. He held a cittern, it looked to Albert much like a miniature guitar, in one hand and hold the other up for attention.

"A song?' he asked, his voice ringing from the rafters.

"A song!" the throng cheered in unison. And with no more ado, the elf began.

I'll tell you a tale, a tale seldom told

*Of people oppressed and a rascal bold Undone by a
queen and her dragon of gold The lion shall lie with
the lamb.
Kochav was queen of a far distant land.
She lived in a palace majestic and grand,
. And Mordechai stood at her right hand.
The lion shall lie down with the lamb*

*Her husband's vizier was an evil old sot, who hated
Kochav and her people a lot.
And conspired to bring them to ruin and rot.
The lion shall lie with the lamb.*

*Though hushed was the talk of the murderous clans
With whom the vizier aimed to scower their lands, The
listening dragon told Kochav their plans.
The lion shall lie with the lamb.*

*Kochav said no this just cannot be.
I'll tell the King. Will he listen to me?
I'll do it at Fest Tide. The people must see.
The lion shall lie with the lamb*

*She begged the King's mercy. Would her words ring true?
Said he, "Rise, Beloved. My trust is in you."
Said she, "Save my people. Without you, we're through.:" The
lion shall lie with the lamb.*

Said the wicked vizier with complexion most sallow,
"Ah few fitter necks would have tested our gallows,"
"None fitter than yours," said the King, "Monsieur Callow."
The lion shall lie with the lamb.

The queen and her dragon had mercifully kept,
Their people alive, both the wise and inept,
And the kindred of Kochav rejoiced as they
wept.
The lion shall lie with the lamb.

"To Kochav and our King!" the bard yelled, raising his tankard high.

"To Kochav and the King!" the tavern replied. The tavern, that is, save for a wrinkled old gnome with hair like a dandelion gone to seed and glasses sitting so low on his nose that they could serve no other purpose than to impress upon others how very intelligent he must be.

"Codswallop!" he yelled in a nasally voice. The inn fell silent.

"Wha's that?" a Minotaur, not Albert's hero, but a shaggy bloke all copper and red, rumbled.

"Ah, ye heard me," the gnome replied. "Cod. Swallop. I'll toast to Kochav; she serves a fine bowl of stew and a palatable enough ale. But the King?" he snorted, "nonsense and tomfoolery."

Kochav had, at that point, threaded her way through he crowd and stood just behind the gnome. Albert go the impression that she'd rather stand in front of him, but alas he was belly up to the bar and rather obstinately refusing to turn.

"Why do you say such things?" she asked.

"Because they're true," he said nasally, his small fist pounding on the bar. "Have any of you seen him these past many years? Or even know someone who has?"

"Aye." Kochav answered quietly. "I see Him in those who help another asking nothing in return. I see Him in those who protect the weak-"

The gnome laughed meanly, fiddling idly with a red and gold ribbon he wore on his lapel. All over the inn, patrons were rising to their feet, pressing inward. Even Malarkey stood on his bench. "Do ye see him too in the sludge that's rotting people from the inside out? In the monsters in the woods? For it's all or nothing, says I; so either he's dead, he's not what we thought him to be or," he took a long pull from his mug, "he never existed at all."

The inn erupted. Voices rang off of the walls, the rafters. Even Mordecai shifted, sending dust and bits of wood raining down from above. Kochav raised her hands.

"Stop!" she ordered. In that moment, in the flashing of her eyes and the voice of someone who expected to be obeyed, Albert saw the queen about whom the bard had sung. She turned back to the gnome; "You'll not say such things here." Her voice was quiet, yet no less resolute for that.

The gnome smiled nastily. "Or what? Ye'll let them pummel me?"

"No," Kochav said, "no one draws in here unless drawn upon. That has been my decree from the start and I'll not change it for the likes of you. But you cannot stay."

"Is me coin not as good then?" the gnome whined.

"There's much that matters more than coin," Kochav replied quietly.

"And what if I don't want to go" the gnome asked, leering, "ye'll throw me out, will ye?"

"Not I," and Kochav nodded towards the door.

Albert had not seen the dwarf from the hearth leave, which, when he thought about it was hardly surprising considering the events of the past few moments. Nevertheless, he must have done for he reentered, followed by a half-dozen penguins dressed in full regalia. Malarkey's caw of alarm was lost in the cheers of the others, and he pushed himself off of the bench with such force that he tangled himself in his cloak, lost his balance, and rolled on the floor.

Sputtering and shaking the dust from his fringe, Malarkey tugged on Albert's sleeve. "Come on, lad, he have to go," he commanded.

Albert was reluctant. "But, I want to-"

"Now!" Malarkey exclaimed. Albert sighed heavily, but gathered his purchase and followed after his friend.

They walked, unhurried and calmly and thus unnoticed, out of a small side door and through a back room that smelled of apples. Albert retrieved Sapphire, and together the trio covered the short distance between the inn and the edge of the Great Wood. There, Malarkey called a halt and then instructed Albert to walk slowly left and then right and left again. With every step the hauberk, rolled up and tucked behind Sapphire's saddle, clinked quietly. On their fourth pass, Albert finally asked what it was they were looking for.

"The path!" Malarkey exclaimed. "There used to be a path here, wide and well-traveled. It was nearly a road!"

"I thought you said you hadn't been here in years,' Albert said.

Malarkey deflated a bit. "Longer than ye've been alive, if ye can believe it." He sighed. "I suppose you're right. Much can change in such a time." The penguin slid off of Sapphire's back and landed with a small thump. "Let's set up camp; we can sort it out in the morning."

Chapter Seventeen

They awoke with the sun. Or, more appropriately, they awoke with the marketplace. The merchants were a rowdy bunch, hallo-ing at one another and boasting or lamenting the previous day's sales as they set up shop. Albert had barely rubbed the sleep sand from his eyes before Malarkey was imploring him to visit the inn for a bit of breakfast. It was on Albert's tongue to ask the bird again why he couldn't do it, but the combination of the look in Malarkey's eyes and the rumbling in Albert's stomach dissuaded him of that notion, and off he went. He entered the inn with not a little bit of apprehension, unsure of what had transpired after they had left the night before. A part of him even thought perhaps the inn would be closed, yet the door swung freely.

Kochav was standing on a bench and attaching a tray of food, presumably Mordechai's breakfast, to some pegs on the wall that seemed to have been placed there for just such a purpose. She turned and smiled warmly.

"Excuse me," Albert said, finding his voice far easier than he had the night before. "Can I ask a question?"

Kochav hopped off of the stool, wiping her hands on her apron. "Yes?" she said, eyebrows raised.

"Can your dragon not leave, or is that the he doesn't?"

Kochav looked over her shoulder at Mordecai. "He's my friend, boy, not my dragon. He is his own dragon. He protected me for many years, at great cost. Now I protect him. He could leave, I suppose, but chooses to stay."

Albert nodded. He wanted to ask more, but the finality in her voice inspired him to let it go. Instead he ordered some rashers, porridge, and a couple of cups of coffee and returned to Malarkey, his tongue poked out of his lips in concentration as he tried not to spill.

They ate in companionable silence, and as they started to pack up, Albert remembered his purchases from the day before, all but forgotten in the excitement.

"Oh!" he exclaimed. "I'm going to go change my clothes," and he ran a few steps into the woods.

It was a blessed relief to peel off the pajamas, though oddly enough Albert found that he could not bring himself to dispose of them and instead he tucked them almost reverently into his satchel. The hauberk was a bit more of a challenge to put on. After not a little bit of twisting, turning, grunting and the occasional "Oof" or "Ouch" he reemerged from the woods. He felt a bit as he used to when his mom would dress him to go play in the snow. His arms stuck out at 45 degree angles and as the hauberk fell to just below his hips, he found himself waddling like, though he would never admit to such a thing, a penguin. Malarkey's fringe danced.

"So, stayed to the shopping list, I see," he said.

Albert flushed and stammered and blushed some more. "Okay but I just thought . . . a hero, and the chordra. And... It was a good deal and. . . . "

Malarkey burst out laughing. "Calm down, lad. You're not the first young man to waste a bit of pocket money on something shiny, nor will you be the last."

Albert's face fell. "Waste? Is it that bad?"

Amusement dancing in his eyes, Malarkey stood and walked to Albert. "Maybe not, let me see." He waddled in a circle around Albert, peering here and there. "It will take work," he said, "cleaning, scrubbing oiling, but perhaps ye can restore it."

"So I can't wear it now?"

Malarkey shook his head. "Patience, lad. 'Tis like most things. Easy enough to buy, harder to earn. Let me help you take it off."

Thus divested of the cumbersome metal, Albert was moving much more freely. They decamped. Albert even had enough time to plait the ribbon he had bought into Sapphire's mane, and it looked quite as nice as he had imagined it would. Sapphire seemed to like it as well, as he whinnied and tossed his head so that the gems sparkled.

As Albert tended to said tasks, Malarkey walked along the wood line. He came back with his brow furrowed.

"Did you find the path?" Albert asked.

"I did. It's overgrown, but it's there. I do no' understand. That was the most travelled route to the south," he said.

Albert countered, "Yes, but years ago."

Malarkey's shoulders slumped. "True. The old path has had use. It just seems that most prefer a different way nowadays."

"So, do we tried to find the road the others are using?" Albert asked. "I can ask around the inn, find out where it is."

Malarkey clicked his beak as he often did when thinking. "Nay, he said at last. There's enough of a path to go by, and a lonelier route might not be the worst idea."

Albert's stomach flip-flopped a bit, looking at the dark trail, and he thought again about asking Malarkey what scared him about meeting others. Instead he swallowed with effort, scratched Sapphire behind his ears, and climbed into the saddle.

"Where exactly are we, anyway?" Albert asked as they rounded the first curve.

"The Great Forest," Malarkey said, something like awe in his voice. "The southern edge. I never thought I'd see it again."

"This is amazing!" Albert exclaimed excitedly. "We are there!"

Malarkey chuckled ruefully. "Not quite lad," he said, "this is no mere copse of trees. This is the greatest wood in the land, in any land." Albert peered into the wood.

"So, how much further do we have to go?" Malarkey sighed.

"We are about halfway there."

Albert's shoulders slumped and he looked down instantly seasick as he watched the ground rise and fall. "We'll never make it" he mumbled.

Malarkey clapped him on the shoulder. "Take heart, young warrior, the battle isn't lost yet."

Deep in the forest, darkness came frustratingly early. Even with the sun at its zenith they moved through a dappled false twilight. The forest was a place of wonder; the soil was moist and loamy and the trees larger than any Albert had ever seen. It fairly teemed with wildlife. Some of the creatures Albert recognized; blue jays still gossiped and scolded noisily in the branches and once they came upon a doe drinking daintily from a pool. Others in the bestiary, though, were every bit as fantastical as the creature they rode. A bright red mammal with one curling horn protruding from the center of its forehead hissed and rattled its ruff when they crashed through the underbrush one evening. Another time, they encountered a mother bird and her five babies. The mother opened her beak and trilled like a flute, the notes warbling up and down the scales as her babies waddled to her on their webbed feet.

If Malarkey grew weary of Albert's constant exclamations, he didn't show it. In fact, he seemed to take a certain joy in granting Albert the knowledge of the creature's true names, monikers somewhat more glorious than "the red horned thing," or "tiny greyeyed furry elephants." Nor did Malarkey's instruction stop at fauna. He imparted on Albert many of the things he learned in Woodcraft, a subject in Gwyythenian, or at least Malarkey's school that meant something quite different than it did from whence Albert came. In Albert's school, woodcraft involved jigsaws and sanders and whatnot. Here, it meant noticing the patterns of moss to determine the direction in which one was travelling, or looking at nothing more than smudges in the path to discern whether or not there were predators in the area. Several times the bird pulled Sapphire up into a stop, only to clamber off and bring Albert back some wildcrafted delicacy. Certain vicious-looking spiky pods were filled with a cottony fruit that tasted as sweet as candy. A low-growing vine with blue flowers was considered sacred by the plainspeople, and used only as a face paint in times of great ceremony, or Great War. Still other plants had medicinal uses, everything from reducing a fever to nourishing a baby animal whose mother had perished. Albert spent a great deal pondering his friend, who seemed to know a bit of everything, and wondering how it was that he'd found himself alone on the Southern Slopes.

"Malarkey," he asked at last, "how do you know so much?"

"It was a long time ago," the bird replied brusquely, and something in his tone told Albert that he should ask no more.

When they stopped for lunch, Albert decided to show off some of what he knew, and gathered several deep-purple berries that looked like the wild raspberries that grew by where Albert and his family used to camp. They were bigger, of course, but it seemed that everything in this strange land was bigger, brighter, and somehow *more* than back home. He collected a biggish amount, more than he could fit in his hand and enough that he pulled up the tail of his shirt, using it as a makeshift pouch. He was hindered, though not unpleasantly, in his task by Sapphire, who insisted upon traipsing along after him. Every couple of steps the horse would stretch his long neck over Albert's shoulder and rest it there, demanding scratches. Albert, of course, was more than happy to comply, rubbing his cheek against Sapphire's own and breathing in the sweet smell of sunlight and hay and horse.

With all of the interruptions, as pleasant as they were, Albert found himself growing both hungry and thirsty. Unable to resist, he raised one of the berries to his mouth and was about to take a bite when a flurry of black and white appeared at the edge of his vision and Albert found himself sprawled on the ground, the berries scattered both hither and yon.

"What are you doing?" Albert asked incredulously.

"Not those, lad, never those," Malarkey panted. "Those will kill you."

"Wh-what?" Albert sputtered. "No they won't. We have those at home." Malarkey climbed, surprisingly gracefully, to his feet and reached his flipper out for Albert.

"This isn't there, boy," he said gently. Albert sighed deeply, wiping the remnants of the berry juice, which had started to tingle at a level just below a sting, off on his pants.

"No," he replied, "I suppose that it's not."

That night, Albert spent a great deal of time currying Sapphire. If all boys treated their animals the way that Albert did his, no beleaguered mother would ever roll her eyes at the begging and promises that so often accompany the acquisitions of such. He brushed the coat until it was gleaming, and all twigs and seeds had been brushed away. He rubbed the horse's shoulders and flanks to work out the soreness, and carefully inspected each hoof for signs of any irritation. He lugged buckets and buckets of cool water from the spring nearby, and when grass was in short supply he would not eat until he'd gathered a large pile of leaves and branches and Sapphire was chomping away. He even tried to make a bed for the beast, out of soft moss, but as the brass pole disallowed Sapphire from lying down, Albert had to satisfy himself with lying as close as he could without being actually underfoot. When at last he'd finished his ministrations, Albert settled in for the night. Sadly, though his body was tired his mind was awake and he spent the first hours of the night plagued with insomnia. Try as he might, he simply could not get comfortable, could not get his busy mind to slow, to settle. He tossed back and forth restlessly.

"What's troubling ye, lad?" Malarkey asked.

"Even the stars are different," Albert replied.

"Do ye still want to go home, then?"

"No... not really. Not anymore," he said, tasting the words as he said them and finding them to be true. "I mean, I miss some things. Like baseball ... and my house ... and my mom, I suppose. Mostly, though, I like it here. I just wished I recognized something ... anything. But I don't. Not even the stars."

"I can help with that," Malarkey said. "There," he motioned with his flipper, "is the goblet and there," pointing at a different part of the sky, "that is the Hunter."

"Orion?" Albert asked, sitting up in his bedroll in excitement.

"I don't know that name, lad, we've always just called him the Hunter. Oh, and that," he said, motioning to a grouping of eleven stars directly ahead, "that is the great turtle, Tukka. There's a fine tale behind that one."

"Will you tell me?" Albert asked, yawning.

He felt, rather than saw, Malarkey smile. "If ye will lie down, and cover up, I will spin ye the tale."

Albert snuggled in, and Malarkey began.

"Long, long ago, when the King had only the wispiest of whiskers on his chin, He spent a great deal of time ranging about His Kingdom. Checking on His people, leading expeditions, fighting off threats. And when He was gone, he would leave His most trusted advisor, a great Wizard, to stand in His place. The Wizard was handsome, as fair as the morning, and he was wise, but deep inside he was plagued by jealousy. As time went on, the Wizard began to feel that he should be leading the Kingdom. He mistook the King's gentleness for weakness, His patience for laziness. And so the Wizard hatched a plan. He began whispering to others of the tyranny of the King, that the King forced His people to obey rules, but that He had none. He spoke of the need for of all Gwytthenia to follow him, that He was more fit to rule, being smarter, braver, and more powerful. He whispered word far and wide that were he the ruler of the Kingdom, those that knelt to him would have all the freedoms they desired. The next time the King was ranging, taking his bravest and truest knights with him, the Wizard made his move. He gathered together those most loyal to his cause and sent them out into the Kingdom, killing all who would not swear fealty. Then, he named himself King, spreading this proclamation far and wide.

The King was gone and his followers had either joined with the Wizard or were huddling, terror-filled, anywhere they could hide. All, that is, except for a wee turtle named Tukka who lived in the castle's gardens. He saw the Wizard marching from the castle and he stumped his way into the middle of the path. As the Wizard approached, Tukka took a deep breath, and as loud as he could he yelled 'You will go no further, villain!'

The Wizard was so taken aback by this act of defiance, that he drew up short. 'Who are you to defy *me*,' the Wizard bellowed. Tukka wanted to withdraw into his shell, and yet he stood firm.

"I am a child of the one true King," he replied, "And I am here to stop you from doing this evil thing."

"You?!?" The Wizard said haughtily. "You are nothing. You are but dirt underneath my feet. What can you do?"

The turtle said, "I cannot do much for I am but a lowly turtle, but I can stand in your way. That much I can do."

Upon hearing this, the Wizard was so furious that they say storm clouds gathered and the sky turned black. He drew back his foot to kick the turtle, a mighty kick that would certainly crush the creature's shell. And yet the turtle didn't move. And so it was that when the Wizard kicked the turtle, the beast grew. He grew and he grew until he turned into a mountain. This mountain ringed the castle gardens, trapping the Wizard inside. Behind that mountain the King was able to rally his forces and return. They cast the Wizard out of the Kingdom forever, as well as those who had joined with him, and order was restored. And so the Kingdom was saved.

"Because of a turtle," Albert murmured sleepily.

"Aye," replied Malarkey, "for even the lowliest of us can stand in the way of evil." The boy was breathing evenly and deep. He was asleep.

Chapter Eighteen

Sapphire's screams, high-pitched and panicked, roused them a few hours later. Albert was on his feet, sword in hand, before he was even awake. His sleep-fogged brain convinced him that the evil wizard from Malarkey's tale had returned to wreak vengeance once again, and his eyes darted this way and that, looking for the tall, lanky man with the tall hat and taller ambition. Moonlight streamed into the clearing, bathing everything in a silvery glow and creating grotesque shadows. Some of the shadows were moving. Albert assumed it was a trick of the light, the moonlight falling through branches dancing in the breeze until a large shadow no more than ten yards away, sprouted spindly legs and took off, scuttling across the glade.

Albert shook his head and suddenly they weren't shadows at all, but spiders. Enormous arachnids poured from the edge of the clearing with bristly hairs and ruby eyes, eight of each clearly visible. The tree trunks were already festooned with their webs, sticky strands of what looked like mummy's wrappings hung everywhere. Several spiders had converged on a single wad of silk and were moving in eerie unison. Pull, rest, grab. Pull, rest, grab. They chittered as they worked, ominous squeaks and grunts that made the hair on the back of Albert's neck stand up. As the bundle neared the top of the trees, it passed through a beam of light, and Albert saw, just for an instant, the gleam of a golden pole.

"Sapphire!" It was meant as a yell, but came out as a whisper. Albert tried again, "*Sapphire!*"

The cocoon began to buck and writhe and Albert could hear the horse, faintly, his whinnies muffled by the strands. That broke his stupor and suddenly the clearing went from dim to bright as Albert's eyes dilated, his teeth bared together in a fearsome grin. He charged into the spiders with a roar that sounded entirely unlike his own voice tearing itself from his throat. One spider's head went rolling and another's carapace was split by Gwytthenian steel, black ichor spraying everywhere. A third found itself scrabbling for purchase as it was fiercely relieved of half if its appendages in one blow. Albert leapt up the tree, scrambling with all of his might, only to fall on the ground. Undeterred, he leapt again. This time, he found himself tangled in the sticky webs. He tore himself free with a barbaric yell, ignoring the red welts that the webbing left on his skin and flung himself still higher. Albert was mere feet away from Sapphire, could almost grab him, when one of the enormous arachnids appeared out of nowhere, it's mandibles clicking. It ignored the boy and headed straight to the horse.

All caution thrown utterly to the wind, Albert climbed on the spider's back, readying his sword for the blow, but the combined weight of the both of them was too much for the silken strands and boy and beast crashed to the ground. Albert's breath was forced out of him in a great whoosh, and he was unable to draw more around the bristly, foul hairs that filled his mouth. Black roses appeared before his eyes. With the last of his strength, Albert angled the sword upward and jerked with all of his admittedly diminished might. The spider squealed and rolled off of Albert. Yanking his sword free, Albert was preparing himself to finish that beast off as well when an alarmed squawk unlike anything he had heard before pierced his brain.

The boy whirled, wiping ichor from his blade, and saw that Malarkey was beset. The penguin lay on his back, his flippers tacked to the ground with webbing, his sword and bow lay impotent by his side. The largest of the spiders reared above him and Albert could see deep amethyst venom dripping from its fangs. Five strides took Albert across the clearing, strides so long he felt as if he was flying. He rolled under the plunging form and thrust his sword upward with all his strength. The spider exploded with the force of the blow, bathing him in hot-stinking fluid. The rest of the beasts scurried off then, taking refuge in the webs among the trees. Albert charged after them, trying to climb webs that pulled and stuck to him, weeping tears he did not feel, scraping his thighs and hands quite badly as he tried to shimmy up the trunks of the trees towards the capsule that no longer moved.

"Come down and fight me!" Albert bellowed. "Come down and fight, you cowards!" He fell again, twisting his ankle painfully and still he tried again.

"Albert," Malarkey yelled, shrill with pain, "it's too late, boy. We have to go."

"No!" Albert was sobbing now, barking sobs that tore at his throat. "I will not. I can save him! I can!" He leapt again, tangling himself for a brief moment that made a spider start forward eagerly until he sliced with his sword and fell to the ground with a thud.

"Help me," Malarkey breathed, and Albert turned. The penguin was panting raggedly, an open wound festered on his breast, and still he was bound to the ground. With one last agonizing look at the bundle of silk that had been his friend, Albert rushed to Malarkey's side. He cut the penguin loose and quickly shoved all of the camp that he could into a sack. Flinging that over one shoulder, he placed Malarkey against his chest, wrapping the bird tight to him with some of their bedding, so that Malarkey was secure but Albert's sword arm was free, and then plunged into the woods adjacent to the clearing. Thirty yards later they found another webbed capsule. Albert's heart leaped, thinking that perhaps the demonic beasts had relented, had returned his friend to him. The webbed mass, however, was much too large to be Sapphire. So large in fact, that it had torn loose from the trees. They could see the loose strands flapping in the breeze. Albert stopped and began hacking awkwardly at the pod.

"What are you doing?" shrieked Malarkey, "That's not your horse!"

"I can stand in the path..." Albert panted, sawing through the strands. "I couldn't save my friend, but I can stand in the path."

A moment later, the capsule parted, releasing a mass of fur and improbable pink feathers. Albert slid on his knees by what he thought was the head of the creature. He pulled the webbing apart to reveal the face of a bear, eyes wild and teeth bared. "Can you move?" Albert asked, "I'll help you, but you have to move."

Slowly, the bear-like creature struggled to his feet, great gobs of drool hanging from his muzzle and his nose nearly touching the ground. The feathers of his great wings dragged in the dirt.

"Jub Jub walk," it rumbled.

"All right," Albert commanded, "let's go." A hundred yards later, the ursine collapsed again, vomiting a stream of foul-smelling bile. Malarkey was asleep, at least Albert desperately prayed he was sleeping, against his chest, and the boy looked around wide-eyed. "I guess it's as good a place as any," he panted, and started to make camp.

After a few false starts, Albert got a fire going. He built it up with one pile of brush after another until it was absolutely roaring. The light of the flames would, he hoped, deter any accomplices that their attackers from earlier may have. He had only managed to grab one tent, and he set that up with the ease of practice. That done, he checked on his companions. Malarkey's wound was now the size of Albert's fist, oozing some noxious fluid, and his eyes were rolled back so far that only a thin line of white was showing. The bear-thing was bleeding from a dozen or more shallow wounds, and one of his legs stuck out at an odd angle. Albert reached out carefully to touch its nose, very aware that his hand was near the fearsome teeth. He remembered that was how you could tell whether a dog was healthy or not, so he took the risk. The nose was dry and hot to the touch.

Desperately, he racked his brain for the lessons that Malarkey had given him. He grabbed a satchel and foraged through the outskirts of camp, unwilling to leave his charges. He gathered some of some yellow-flowered moss that Malarkey had once pointed out, as well as a bark that, if he remembered right, helped with fever, and another that he thought helped with pain. Frightened, his heart pounding in his chest, he even went back to where he had cut the bearcreature free and gathered some of the cast aside webbing. He remembered reading once that spider webs could be used to make wounds clot. His bag bulging, he returned to camp. Malarkey was breathing so shallowly that for one terrifying moment Albert thought him dead.

"Oh no," he moaned, sliding to his knees beside his friend. "Oh no, oh no." He laid his head on the downy breast and was kneeweakeningly relieved to feel the rise and fall of his breath. Albert covered the wound liberally with the moss, and was encouraged to see the flowers start to brown as the poison was leached out. Malarkey had told him that such discoloration was the way to tell if the moss was working. He thgen tried to force the bark and plants down his patients' throats, but they were too weak to chew. Desperate to do something, Albert placed the plants in a pot with a bit of water and set it above the flames.

Albert heard a rustling in the leaves and whirled about in panic, certain the spiders were back. The bear-thing was seizing, his paws paddling, claws scoring great divots in the ground. Albert heard somewhere, he wasn't sure where, that you had to put something in the mouth if someone started seizing, to stop them from swallowing their tongue. He found a stick, more like a small branch, and shoved it between the creature's teeth. The enormous canines clamped down, splintering the stick almost instantly. Instinctively, Albert reached for the slivers before the beast could choke on them. At the last moment, he jerked his hand back, narrowly missing an impromptu amputation. Finally, the violent movement subsided. A hissing and splattering sound let Albert know that the tincture was boiling, sending little drops of liquid out of the pot to sizzle on the burning logs. Albert ran to the fire and set the pot on the ground to cool.

As he did, he noticed that the moss on both creatures was sodden, brown, and nauseating. Wiping sweat from his brow and already exhausted, he ran to gather more of the yellow-flowered flora. Pulling the used moss off of the wounds was disgusting. It smelled of rotten meat and was slimy to the touch. Albert had to stop several times to heave dryly into the dirt, but finally it was all removed. The wounds were still festering, green and purple around the edges and so he packed them again. Finally, he was able to get some of the tincture down his wards' unresisting throats and collapsed shakily onto his backside.

Albert did not believe he had dozed off, did not think that such a thing would be possible, and yet when Malarkey started screaming, he found himself jolted to awareness. Albert sprang to the bird's side and felt his forehead. Even through the feathers, he was burning hot yet shivering. Albert changed the moss yet again, and administered more tincture. Then, he held the bird close, rocking him, singing the little bits of lullabies that he remembered from his infancy. By morning, the bear had seized one more time, Malarkey still shivered, and Albert had nearly given up hope. He noticed, once the clearing was light once more, that the moss was slower to brown. He thought the wounds looked better as well, less angry, but that might have been his imagination.

"Please, please, please," Albert found himself whispering. He couldn't get farther than that, there was too much to ask for, and so he just hoped that the One to whom he spoke would know the rest. "Please, please, please."

At some point, Albert didn't remember quite when, he switched from moss to spider webs, hoping to stem the red tide seeping out of his charges and into the ground.

Later, he made another trip back to where they were attacked. Luckily, their supplies were still where he'd left them, and Albert gathered them together with arms that felt heavy and sluggish. He scanned the treetops for signs of Sapphire, but there were none. Suddenly, a flash of color caught his eye, and Albert ran over. It was Sapphire's ribbon, covered with bits of web and crumpled sadly. Albert fell to his knees, carefully wiping the ribbon clean. "I'm so sorry," he whispered, holding it up to his nose and breathing in the horsey smell. "I'm so sorry." After a few moments, he wiped his face and headed back to camp.

Albert was busy cutting a blanket into strips to use for bandages when he realized he was squinting. He rubbed his eyes, trying to remove the sleep-sand. It didn't help. Thunder rumbled, close, and only then did Albert realize that the dimness came not from him, but from the rushing and roiling clouds overhead. He groaned, palming at his face, and leapt to his feet. Malarkey was easy enough to tend to, Albert simply scooped him up and carried him into the tent. The ursine, however, was more of a problem. Adrenaline and energy depleted, Albert simply could not budge him. Not that he would have fit in the tent in any case. Finally, desperate, Albert took the ropes and hung the tent and a blanket as a sort of canopy above the bear. He was tying the last rope as lightning crashed overhead and the skies opened.

Within an hour, Albert had given up any pretense of staying dry. He moved in a constant triangle, from bird to bear to fire, where he fought valiantly to keep the flames burning so that he could make more of the tincture. Whether it was helping or not, he was not sure, but it wasn't hurting and so he was unwilling to allow his companions to miss a dose.

As the ground became sodden, so did the winged bear. Malarkey's feathers of course, kept him dry, but his bandages quickly became a soggy mess and so Albert changed them until there were no more strips of blanket left, pulling the least wet ones off from above the fire and reapplying them with increasingly numb fingers. The rain continued through the next day as Albert staggered around camp in a stupor, blinded by exhaustion, kept conscious only by the pervading fear that if he slept, only for a moment, the other two would surely die. So tired was he, that he didn't notice when the rain stopped, only that he was, gradually, less miserable. He thought that the bird's forehead and the other beast's nose felt cooler, though still dry, so dry. Albert gave them water from a cup, a dribble at a time, as the constellations – turtle and cup, the Lady and the wand, appeared overhead.

As the sun rose on the third morning, the golden light stabbing into Albert's gritty eyes, both Malarkey and Jub Jub were awake. Albert changed their dressings mechanically, murmuring a constant stream of encouragements. He set some water by each of them.

"I'm going to sleep now. Gotta. Jus' a few minutes. Wake me up if you need anything. Promise?" Malarkey nodded, and the bear creature lifted his head. Albert jumped back, not sure how the beast would react now that it was awake. It looked at him with limpid eyes.

"Jub Jub ... promise," he rumbled, and Albert relaxed.

"All right, that's good then." He staggered over to his bedroll and was asleep before his head hit the ground.

Chapter Nineteen

The sun had barely moved before Albert opened his eyes once again. His body as stiff and sore, complaining, and his mouth was woolly. He panicked for a moment when he tried to sit up and could not, before he realized that he was covered by a dense blanket of bright pink feathers. Albert rolled away and the feathers retreated.

"Boy cold," a voice said.

"Yeah, I was, thanks." Albert rose, slowly and painfully, to his feet, and relieved himself at the edge of the clearing. Walking more easily by then, he sat next to the fire. It was crackling merrily, the golden flames dancing in the morning light. Malarkey was tending to the blaze. He moved jerkily, wobbling two and fro like a wind-up toy, but he was moving. Albert grabbed a water skin and drank thirstily. "You're alive," he croaked ingeniously. "You're both alive."

"Aye we are, lad," the penguin replied. "Thanks to you." Albert opened his mouth to say something pithy, nonchalant, but instead he burst into tears.

Many moments passed before the tears finally subsided. At some point in the torrent, Jub Jub lumbered over and laid his enormous head in Albert's lap. Albert stroked the coarse fur while Malarkey patted the boy's shoulder awkwardly with his flipper.

"I'm sorry," Albert sniffled at last, scraping at his eyes and leaving a smear of mud. "I was just so scared."

"Even so, you did well," Malarkey reassured.

"Everyone get scared," Jub Jub murmured. Albert drank again. The skins were nearly empty. He would have to fill them soon, and he would. In just a few moments, he would.

"How long was I asleep?" he asked. "It felt like forever, but the sun barely moved."

"A night and a day," Malarkey replied. Albert leapt to his feet.

"You should have woken me," he chided. "The spiders could have come back ... your medicine ... the fire!"

"You needed the sleep," Malarkey replied. "Well fashed, ye are. We were able to manage."

"Boy tired," Jub Jub said. Albert reached out and scratched the being behind his ears. The creature leaned into it, his eyes half-closed.

"Albert," Albert told him. "That's my name."

"Albert," the thing repeated. "Jub Jub."

"Nice to meet you, Jub Jub," Albert said, then headed off to get water and ingredients to make breakfast. He was ravenous.

The woods that morning were more alive than Albert had ever seen them. The underbrush rustled with movement, the ground was dappled with the forms of figures flying overhead. The path itself was getting positively worn, far from the beaten down bit of grass it had been. Everyone and everything was going in the same direction. North, north, always north, Albert could almost hear it as a heartbeat. By midday, Albert had seen a fearsome group of ogres covered in lumps and warts and grunting amongst themselves, a sinewy purple tiger, lithe women in diaphanous gowns with crowns of leaves that Malarkey identified as dryads, and countless flying folk that were little more that sparks of light among the clouds.

"Going to the festival," Jub Jub said, eyeing the creatures in flight with longing.

"You can go too if you want to," Albert said, secretly hoping that he wouldn't. Obviously kind and gentle-natured, Jub Jub was still large enough, especially his gigantic claws, to deter any malevolent being that they might encounter. Beyond the simple matter of survival, Albert enjoyed snuggling up to him at night, buried in both fur and wing. He laughed at the bear's comical faces as he slurped up berries delicately, one by one, and the look or surprise when the woodland stew was too hot. Jub Jub unfurled his wings and Albert gasped; he had drastically underestimated the size of them, and he stood perfectly still as the bear-thing beat the huge pink appendages rapidly. The trees at the edge of the clearing bent outward, but the huge padded paws remained rooted firmly to the ground.

"Not ... strong ... yet," Jub Jub panted, sadly. Albert patted him on the paw, and then starting mixing and cooking a giant pot of woodland stew from mushrooms, wild garlic, and some beautifully spiraled fiddleheads he was lucky enough to find in a shady patch of ground. He was actually getting quite good at cooking, at least over a campfire (he had a sneaking suspicion that in a real kitchen sandwiches and macaroni and cheese would still be his forte), and while several creatures stopped to partake of a bowl, none stayed long. They were cordial enough, jovial, but obviously in a hurry to be on their way. Albert's heart ached to go with them, and he would watch them until they disappeared around the curve in the path, filled with a yearning that he could not quite identify, though clearly Malarkey and Jub Jub felt the same.

Still, they remained at the campsite, glancing lingeringly to the north and cursing the spiders for their devastation and heartlessness. Jub Jub kept trying to fly, and by the second morning he could make short hops. He and Albert made a game of it, chasing after colorful butterflies as they flitted from one flower to the next in the glade. On one of those jaunts, Jub Jub's nose started to twitch. His nostrils grew huge, and he began to salivate. Albert stepped back slowly, eyes wide. "What is it?" he asked. "Rattletails? Wolves? Another Chordra?"

"Honey," Jub Jub grumbled. Sniffing loudly, Jub Jub meandered through the woods until they found a large, hollow tree. Albert knocked on it. It gave back an echoing boom, followed by an angry buzzing not unlike a mob of little old ladies all chattering together. Jub Jub tried to fly to the hole in the trunk, tantalizing them about fifteen feet off of the ground, but the trees were too close together for him to get any sort of lift and he collapsed into an ungainly pile of limbs again and again.

"It's okay," Albert consoled him. "Let's just go back to camp." Jub Jub's lower lip protruded and Albert bit back a laugh. He had never seen a bear pout before.

"But ... honey," he said, morosely. Albert chewed on his lower lip and stared at the hole. He thought that he could even see the golden liquid inside, but it might have been the light of the sun. Still, saliva squirted into his mouth.

"All right," he said at last. "Let me stand on your shoulders." Jub Jub looked at him dubiously. "Just trust me," Albert said. Still with his nubs of eyebrows raised, Jub Jub nodded.

"Jub Jub trust Albert," he said. He lay on the ground, and not without quite a bit of effort, Albert clambered up.

"Now, walk to the tree," Albert said, "and stand up." The bear followed directions, and Albert got shakily to his feet, shimmying to and fro. He leaned heavily against the tree trunk, grimacing as his stomach scraped painfully against the bark. He stretched up on his toes, then yelped and he started to tip backward. Jub Jub leaned, trying to help but they overcorrected and Albert bumped his nose. "I can't ... quite ... reach," he groaned, sticking his tongue between his lips in concentration.

He regretted that decision almost instantly as Jub Jub suddenly jolted upwards with the sound of claws on bark, and Albert's teeth snapped together on his tongue. Another jolt. Jub Jub was panting, and Albert realized that they were climbing the tree. He laughed wildly, imagining how they must look. One more jolt and he could reach into the hole. He did so slowly, gingerly. A couple of bees flew out, buzzing just in front of his face.

He could see their multi-lensed eyes and did his best to hold perfectly still, to look inconspicuous. After a long moment, the bees flew away, and Albert once again began inching his hand inside the hole. Finally, his fingers reached something firm and sticky. He dug his fingers in, while the buzzing inside intensified. A sharp pain shot up his arm and he yelped. As if that were a signal, he found himself surrounded by angry striped insects. One of the soldiers found Jub Jub's nose and the bear-creature roared, pushing them off from the tree and flapping his wings wildly to slow their descent. Albert fell backwards, straight into a fluffy cushion of fur just before they hit the ground. Their chastisement complete, and with pollen to gather and honey to replenish the bees thankfully gave up pursuit.

Albert and Jub Jub lay on the ground, mentally cataloguing their wounds. Five stings, a couple of bruises, and one dripping fistful of honey. Back at camp, Malarkey was able to make a paste that took the pain out of the stings and as they ate griddle cakes made from ground up acorns and smeared with honey the vote was unanimous.

It had been absolutely worth it.

"My mom used to make us honey and biscuits every Sunday when ... when my dad was home," Albert said.

"My ma would do the same, before a long day of training," Malarkey replied. "What about you, Jub Jub?" Albert asked, licking his hands. The bear rested his head on his paws.

"Jub Jub no mother," he said forlornly.

"Well, what about you dad?" Jub Jub shook his head slowly. "Brothers? Sisters?" Albert persisted. A large tear fell from Jub Jub's eyes.

"Jub Jub only Jub Jub. All alone." Albert flung himself across the clearing, wrapping his arms around the creature and smearing honey in his fur.

"Not anymore."

Chapter Twenty

The next morning, perhaps fortified by honey, but more likely by the unrestrained hug that Albert had given him the night before (for as you know, a good hug can cure many an ill) Jub Jub spread his wings and tried flying again. With much grunting and straining his feet first slid across the ground and then flirted with it, grazing and departing like a butterfly among wildflowers. Finally, the great claws left the ground entirely, if only for a meter. Albert broke into shouts and cheers of congratulations, and even Markey, who had been spending the morning meticulously maintaining their supplies, cleaning and sharpening daggers, mending bed rolls, and such, looked up and nodded in approval.

Laughing, Albert ran over and tapped Jub Jub lightly on the shoulder. "Tag, you're it!" he yelled, and sprinted to another part of the clearing.

Jub Jub just stared at him, puzzled and blinking.

"You have to come and get me," Albert exclaimed through giggles, "You're it! You have to fly and catch me!"

The bear's furrowed brow melted into a toothy grin and then a frown of concentration as he flapped his wings once more. No sooner had he caught up with Albert, bumping the boy with his huge, shaggy head than Albert sprinted away once more. Their game took them merrily though the woods, far beyond the places they had previously explored as Albert sprinted further away, or climbed an obliging tree, or scrambled the top of a rock pile. Eventually, he saw the greatest challenge of all, a craggy rock face rising about ten feet above the ground, Panting and sweating, Albert climbed to the top and then yelped, pinwheeling his arms for balance.

The top of the rocks were both narrow and wet, surrouning a crisp, clear pool of water that was bubbling with the force of the waterfall crashing into it at the far end. Jub Jub, breathing heavily with the effort, landed beside Albert and patted him with a leathery paw.
"Albert. . . it."

"Oh yeah?" Albert laughed, "What about this?" He knelt down and scooped up water, splashing it at Jub Jub, whose eyes widened as he licked the droplets from his muzzle. His retaliation, fully expected and eagerly anticipated, was also underestimated and the resulting wave sent Albert flying backwards into the pool. It was delightfully cool and bubbly, and before long both the bear and boy were swimming.

Their frivolity took them even closer to waterfall, which was, while rather wide, not incredibly tall nor fierce, formed as it was by ice melt higher in the mountains. As Albert floated on his back he stared, mesmerized by the falling water. After a few moments, he realized that he bluish lights that he took to be the reflection of the sun off of the water appeared instead to be coming from the rocks behind. Albert motioned to Jub Jub and the pair sidestepped along the rocks that lined the pool, tentatively inching closer and closer to the blue light. Albert found himself reaching towards his waist, grasping for the sword that unfortunately still sat at camp. He cursed himself thrice for a fool. If Malarkey had told him once, he had told him a million times, the very nature of danger was that it was unexpected, thus one must always be prepared.

"Well, I didn't intend to find any danger, "Albert defended himself in his head.

"We rarely do," Imaginary Malarkey answered.

The closer they got to the falls, the brighter the light grew, until Albert found himself having to squint to see. Suddenly, he stopped, chewing his lip, and turned around. "I think. . . " he said, "I think we'd better go and get Malarkey."

Albert expected Malarkey to be irritated with him, but instead the bird seemed to be relieved. If you have been ill for any length of time, then perhaps you also understand that the thought of getting to do nothing and the reality of having to do nothing are two very different things. Malarkey, being a man, well, *bird* of action, was getting very tired of both thought and deed. Albert grabbed his sword and in no time it all, it seemed, they were back at the falls.

Albert was starting to creep his way along the edge once again when Malarkey held a flipper up to beak, winkled, and dove into the water. Albert had never seen Malarkey swim before, and his mouth fell into an "o" of delighted surprise. The penguin did well enough on land of course, the generations-old gifts from the Prince and years of training saw to that, but this, Albert saw at once, this was his home. Malarkey burst from the water like a wee torpedo from one end of the pool, peeped at the waterfalls, and disappeared, only to emerge somewhere wholly different. After a dozen or so of these passes Albert saw him slide under the falls and leap to the rocks behind.

Seconds later, Malarkey was back. "Come. Run." he said, and dove again into the bubbling water.

"Danger?" Jub Jub asked.

"No," Malarkey replied. "Tis the opposite of danger. 'Tis a doorway to the castle itself! "

No sooner were the words out of his beak than Albert and Jub Jub were half-running, half-slipping on the rocks grinning from ear to ear to where the rock face curved back on itself behind the falls, creating a cozy cave. Water droplets clung to every surface, giving back light like diamonds.

Malarkey stood awestruck in front of a swirling white blue fog. "Here!" he breathed. "It's . . . right . . . here!"

Slowly, his heart pounding in his chest and his eyes fixed in equal parts fear and excitement, Albert moved to stand beside his friend. The boy took a deep breath and blew it out slowly between pursed lips the way that his dad had taught him to do when he was afraid of speaking in front of his class. Slowly he gazed into the center of the light, and then stepped back in shock.

"Do ye see it? The tapestries, the stone?" Malarkey asked.

"No," Albert said breathlessly. "I see Samuel's room. It has blue walls and bookshelves. Home! It's my way home!"

"Let me look again," Malarkey said, and peered into the mist. "No, lad, that's the castle. Look to the right. That's the emblem of the King."

"That's not what I see at all!" Albert said. He was close to tears. "To the right is the window with the old oak tree!"

Malarkey stepped back from the portal, clicking his beak in frustration. "Jub Jub," he commanded, "come look."

The bear-creature ambled over amicably enough. As he passed Albert, his shoulder bumped the boy who fell towards the slight.

"Careful!" cawed Malarkey.

Albert threw himself back past Jub Jub's rump, and looked at him in anticipation. "What do you see?" he asked. "

"Jub Jub see clouds . . . cave . . . home."

Suddenly alarmed, Malarkey stepped back, doing his best to shoo the other's away from the bluish light. "Get back! I don't' know what kind of magic this is, but me da' always said not to trust any non-living thing that can read your mind."

Slowly, carefully, Albert walked around the swirling mist. From the side it looked like a thin line, like light coming through a cracked door. When he walked behind it, he was treated to a view of his friends staring toward, though not at, him. Back to the front and he was looking into Samuel's room once again. "It's a portal!" he exclaimed.

"Por. . tal?" Jub Jub asked.

"Tex told us about them!" "

He also said they'd gotten dangerous," Malarkey countered.

"He said getting to one was dangerous," said Albert. "And it was! The spiders. . ." he shuddered, "but we are here now! We found one!"

Malarkey stood for a long time, considering. "Ye may be right," he said at last. "I've heard tell of such magic doorways. Still, it's not much farther to the castle. If it's all the same, lad, I'd like to go on by foot."

"But I don't want to go to the castle anymore!" Albert exclaimed. "I was only going there so that I could go home!" "But the King-" Malarkey began.

"The King was just my way home, " Albert interrupted.

Malarkey's head jerked back as though he'd been struck, and even Jub Jub looked astonished and not a little disappointed.

"Just?" Jub Jub echoed.

Malarkey shook his head. "Still? Even after everything you've heard that's all you think He is?"

"Those are your stories. Your history. Not mine! There's nothing here of mine!" Albert's voice was harsher than he intended, and hot tears rose in his eyes.

Jub Jub's head fell and his massive shoulders slumped.

"So that's the way of it, then," Malarkey said evenly.

Albert ran his hand through his hair. "I. . . I don't know, okay! I don't know. All I know is that I don't belong here."

"Do you not?" Malarkey asked quietly. "I'm not so sure."

The water, pouring and frothing, did it's best to fill the silence as the trio stood, appealing to one another with their eyes and, excruciatingly slowly, understanding that no matter how much they wished it, no agreement could be found.

Malarkey sighed. "All right. It's your choice."

He stood before the boy, shuffling his feet. His flippers raised from his sides a few times, and then fell again, as though he was going to embrace Albert. Finally, though, he just turned away. Jub Jub, on the other hand, had no such reservations, and his furry head thudded into Albert's chest.

As Albert wrapped his arms around him, the first tears fell from his eyes onto the beast's fur. "I'll miss you," Albert murmured.

Wordlessly, Jub Jub turned and followed Malarkey down the rocky side of the pool. Albert watched them until they were out of sight.

When even the branches through which they'd disappeared stopped moving, Albert took a deep breath and turned back to the portal. He took one step, then another. One more would take him through. He lifted his foot, and then paused. Samuel's room, well, it was Samuel's. It wasn't his, not really. By this time he was more of a stranger there than he was in Gwytthenia. There was a celling blocking out the stars. He could see headlights from passing cars cutting through the dark. Albert took a step back. He looked over his shoulder, searching for his friends. He missed them already. Of course, he missed his mom, too. He stepped forward again. Just one more step. One more and there would be no more spiders. No more ick. No more chordras or mystery. Forward. No more Jub Jub or Malarkey or Tex or Ahoka. More than that he was afraid that he'd leave a bit of himself behind; the part that could ride horses – at home he had been afraid of horses. The part that could nurse people back to health. The part that could, maybe, be a hero. Back. He didn't know how long he'd been gone. His mom might be worried. She might need a hero, too. Forward. But if he went back, he'd never know why he'd been brought here to begin with. He'd never be a hero.

Albert crouched down, wrapping his pounding head in his hands. "Graaaaahhh!!!" he yelled. The cave sent it back to him in an echo. Albert remembered lying in bed, sandwiched between his mom and dad in their giant bed in another new home. He was sad. He'd missed their old house.

"Don't you know?" his mom said. "Home is where the heart is."

Where was his heart? What did it want? Albert thought he knew. Maybe. He bent over, picked up a rock, and kissed it.

"Love you, mom," he said, and threw the rock though the portal. The blue light grew brighter, so bright the Albert had to cover his eyes with his arm. When he uncovered his eyes, the portal was gone. "I'll be back as soon as I can," he said to the place where it had been.

The moon was high by the time Albert reached camp. He was toe-stepping so as not to wake up his companions. When he arrived, however, the fire was still crackling and Malarkey and Jub Jub were sitting, unusually close to one another, in front of it. They raised their heads in unison as he approached. Albert opened his mouth, but no words came. He shrugged. Malarkey nodded back and Jub Jub scooted over a bit, making room. Albert snuggled between them gratefully and sniffled a bit, wiping his nose on his sleeve. Jub Jub laid his head in Albert's lap.

"I'm proud of you, "Malarkey said, not taking his eyes off of the fire. "That was brave. Braver, mayhap, than I would have been." "Do you think I made the right decision?" Albert asked.

"Do you?" said the bird.

Albert poked at the fire with a stick, sending sparks up into the heavens. "I do," he said, both surprised and relieved to discover that he believed it. "I really think I do."

Chapter Twenty One

Albert woke late the next morning to find Malarkey hurriedly stowing pots and pans, rolling up bedding, and dousing the fire.

"It's time, Lad,' the bird said. "We may make it for the end if not the beginning. It's better than nowt."

Albert went to Jub Jub, checking his wounds. They were healed; the scars would remain, but all in all the flesh had knitted nicely.

"Are you sure you'll be okay?" he asked. "It's a long walk."

"No walk, fly."

"Oh." Albert's face fell and he busied himself with making sure the fire was indeed out and the ashes scattered, desperately hoping that no one would see the tears in his eyes. Soon the clearing held little sign of their stay. He had hoped that the trio would continue their journey together. He understood, of course. Why would anyone walk if they could fly? Still, it hurt.

Finally, he could put it off no longer. He flung his arms around Jub Jub's neck, burying his face in the pleasant smell of dust and sunlight. "Goodbye, then, Jub

Jub. I'll miss you." Jub Jub's nose drooped until it was nearly touching the ground, and large tears gathered in his brown eyes.

"G-goodbye?" he asked.

"Yeah," Albert said, his voice croaking. "We have to go ... I don't want to, but I have to ... So ... it's time to leave. It's a long walk," he said.

"Walk?" Jub Jub's shoulders drooped still further. "You no think Jub Jub fly good?"

Albert's eyes widened. "No!!" he said, shaking his head. His brow was furrowed in confusion. "I'm sure you are a very good flyer." "You ... you no like Jub Jub?" Desperately, Albert looked to Malarkey for help, but the bird was not in the clearing.

"We like you a lot!" Albert exclaimed. "It's just that, we can't fly and-"

"A ridiculous oversight I've thought," Malarkey said, rejoining them.

"No ride?" Jub Jub asked.

Finally, finally, Albert understood. "Wait! You want us to ride on you?"

Jub Jub nodded forlornly as tears dripped into the earth. Albert looked at Malarkey who nodded, something like a grin on his face. "We'd love to! Can you do it?"

Jub Jub's head came up immediately, his mouth open in a wide toothy smile of joy. "Jub Jub can!" he said. "You ride?" "Yes!" Albert said through laughter. "We'll ride!"

* * *

Any illusions that Albert may have had about soaring gracefully through the firmament evaporated once they tried to clamber aboard Jub Jub's broad back. Malarkey tried thrice, sliding to the ground with a thump each time, before he deigned to allow Albert to lift him. With the bird nestled in the thick fur, it was Albert's turn. The boy dug his fingers in the pelt and pulled, wincing as he kicked his friend in the ribs. Jub Jub didn't seem to mind, his mouth remained smilingly open. Once the passengers were finally seated and their gear secured, Jub Jub began to gallop across the clearing. Albert's head wobbled like a doll's and his teeth clacked like castanets. The enormous wings unfurled. They began flapping powerfully but almost painfully slowly. The trees rushed towards them at an alarming speed, and Malarkey let out a squawk of pure terror. Albert scrunched his eyes shut as the tree line rushed towards them. It seemed that gravity would never relinquish its hold. Then, suddenly, they were free. The sun, unhindered by leaves, beat down on them and the spine-jarring flaps evened out. The air was crisp and clear and blew Albert's hair, longer and shaggier than it had ever been, out of his eyes. Albert let out a whoop of sheer delight, his fish punching the air. Jub Jub answered with a growling laugh, and they were on their way.

Jub Jub couldn't fly for long that first day as his strength was still returning. Even so, the distance they covered was nothing less than phenomenal. Even the terrain was different. Moss grew in a thick carpet, and wild brambles dropped, nearly touching the ground with the weight of their fruit. Albert gathered several handfuls of the latter while Malarkey made camp. As the bird tended to dinner, the boy rubbed the soreness out of Jub Jub's shoulders.

The next morning they were off by sunrise. Jub Jub was much improved already. He delighted Albert, if not Malarkey, with a series of banks and dives and, once, a heart-stopping loop the loop. Late in the afternoon, lulled by the warmth of the sun, Albert laid back across Jub Jub and fell asleep, rocked by the beating of the wings. That nap was the sleep against all others would be measured and found wanting for the rest of his life. Malarkey woke him as the sun went down, and the trio's eyes sparkled as orangey-rose and golden lights caressed them.

Malarkey became disturbingly morose and withdrawn when they landed, however. His mood deepened as night went on, and Albert could hear him muttering to himself. As their campfire grew larger, sending sparks into the already starry sky, they could hear the first beats of drums, distant, like the heartbeat of a giant. Malarkey's shoulders drooped and he kept glancing, furtively, to the North.

Albert assumed that Malarkey was disappointed to be missing the start of the Great Feast. "We should be there tomorrow, right?" He asked encouragingly. Malarkey said nothing, only nodded. Albert stared in puzzled excitement at the flames, while Jub Jub dozed, snoring quietly nearby. After a moment, the boy tried again. "But everyone will still be there, right? I mean, it lasts quite a while" Malarkey stayed as silent as the grave, nodding again. "What's wrong?" Albert asked at last. Malarkey's body started to shake, and after a moment Albert realized to his chagrin that he was crying.

"Build up the fire," the bird said, "and I'll spin ye a tale" he said in his squeaky voice. "Just promise," his voice cracked, "promise you won't hate me."

Malarkey began. "There was never a time, not in all me life, that I didna want to be a knight," the bird began. "I was born in the royal hatchery, just like my father and his father before him, way back many and many-a. My first memory is of being presented, along with the rest of the hatchlings, to the King and Prince themselves. Ah it was a glorious day and all the wee ones covered in down, tryin' not to shuffle our feet or wiggle around. Me mum and da presented me, told them my name and line and a bit about what they'd noticed about me. The King gazed down on me. I just remember his eyes, clear and blue as a summer sky and how I felt warm all over, as if the sun had just come out from behind a cloud. He patted my wee head and the Prince spoke low, quietly, to my folks. I didn't hear what he said, by my da ruffled his feathers and stood up straight and tall as a mountain and me ma hugged me close with tears in her eyes. That night, they told me I'd been chosen to be part of the Kings' guard. My da pulled down the family book and showed me all of my ancestors who had served before me. Once we'd gotten to the end, we wrote my name. Macauley Declan O'Cannon. It was the proudest moment of me life.

Soon, I started me educations. A knight, ye must know, learned far more than reading and math. We studied the great history of Gwytthenia, combat, chivalry. Me best mate was a lad named Donovan. His parents were neither one working in the castle, commoners ye see, though of a noble line as all penguins are. He got a lot of guff for that. One day I caught a group of youngsters roughing him up, calling him names and what like. I sailed into battle and next I knew one of the hooligans was bleeding from a cut on his chest and another was missing a great tuft of feathers. The others turned and ran. We were punished by the headmaster, though it was not as bad as it could be as he knew the troubles Don had been having. That night as we lay in our bunks we became blood brothers. 'If you ever need anything,' he said, 'Just call. I'll be there. Anytime, anywhere.'

When we got older, we left our book studies behind, and training got even harder. They took us into these very woods once, bare as a bunch of hatchlings and with not even a water skin or flint and steel and told us that we'd have to find our way back. It took me over a week before I came dragging in, nowt but feathers and mud and yet I was still better off than most. Some lads hadna been able to make fire, the wood being so wet. Another had slipped and fallen and broken a leg. Worst of all, one of my classmates had crawled into a cave without knowin' it was a winter den for rattletails. We searched for three days before we brought him home and buried him proper.

With honors, of course. He was the first among us to be knighted.

We had to learn to work with all sorts of creatures, and so they sent us in ones and twos to live all over our land. I lived with the centaurs and learned to read the stars and the power of silence. I lived with dwarves deep in the mines, and got to know how they settled disputes by community votes. Once, I spent a month in the islands where it was so warm that I started molting. Came back puffed out like a field flower gone to seed and sunburn on me beak. By the time we reached our knighting ceremony there were only six of us from my hatching that were left. I kneeled before my King at a great ceremony, part of the very fest we will attend, and was knighted Sir Macauley of Gwytthenia.

Ah, then started the bonniest time o' me life. I spent me days having grand adventures; competing in jousts, guarding the agates, once I even had to deliver a message to the Plainspeople from the King, Himself. I found meself a colleen and she was as fair as the morning, her back was as black as coal, her breastfeathers as white as snow, and her fringe feathers curled a little at the ends, making her look surprised, especially if she had just woken up. We started courting, and once, after I'd had a grand day in the lists, wearing her favor, I even managed to unhorse me pal Donovan, she let me kiss her.

She had hatched in the brood after mine, and was apprenticed to the royal weaver. Everyone said she showed great promise. Her colors were richer than anyone had even seen and the stories she could tell with bats of yarn, ah they'd make you weep. Everyone expected us to be married by spring, and in truth I'd already spoken to her da. To get his blessing. I was just waiting for the right moment, when I felt like I could be the husband she deserved.

Then, it was my turn to patrol the outer wall. We would be assigned to the outers for three months at a time, and the assignment either went to the very new knights, those still earning their mettle, or the very old, those who were no longer as hale and strong as they had once been. The outers were far from the castle, rough-like, but there hadn't been a major threat there in over a century, so there was little real danger. The guard duty was mostly to remind us that there were those who didn't often see the King in person. We needed them to know that he was very much still in power and there foe them. Shortly into my deployment, I befriended a raggle-taggle groups of youngsters whose 'territory' ran nearby my post. They fancied themselves a 'gang.'" Malarkey scoffed.

"I didn't believe it of them. King help me, I didn't believe. They just seemed young, barely out of the egg, and lost and they told such well-crafted stories. One spoke of parents who spent their days in the taverns and their nights quarreling at home. Another spoke of his mother, who died after a long illness, leaving him with nothing. Being thrown out of their homes, forced to live on the streets. I didn't know then if any of it was true; I don't know now. But by the end of my deployment, I thought of them as friends. I wanted to help them. Ever the knight, I suppose. In any case, I spoke to some friends, called in some favors and got the 'gang' jobs in the castle. Then I went home, patting myself on the back for a job well done. The problems started almost immediately.

    There were tales of churlishness, of not showing up to work. People would ask me to talk to them, so of could I would. They always had a reason, would always promise, tearfully, to do better. And they would, for three-four days, maybe even a week, and then the shenanigans would begin again. When we were all off duty, we would go to town, talking, laughing, drinking. They would stroke my ego. I'll admit it now. Among the other knights, I was little more than a squire. Not the top o' my class, not the bottom. But, among the fellows from the outers, I was nearly royalty. I was their benefactor. I could mount a horse and speak seven languages. I had spoken to the King, Himself. They fed me compliments along with cake and ale and I ate it all. Soon, me lass Jardine became scared, then angry. She confronted me about it once, it tears. 'They're talking about you Macauley, everyone is. They say you've changed and I say so, too.' I promised I'd clean up my act, spend more time with her, but alas I was no better at keeping my promises than my new 'friends.'

It got so bad that my Captain called me to his quarters. 'I've seen it before, lad, many times, but I never believed such of you.' That should have been enough. Would have been were I not so blind. Still, I stood up for them. I promised on my name, on my *name,* that they were as trustworthy as I." He threw a stick into the fire with such venom that a slew of sparks shot outward.

"A few weeks later, I was on guard duty for the treasury, the vault where the Kingdom's most treasured jewels were kept. The Captain had tried to trust me, a little at least. Most of my classmates, however, were out of their first Expedition with the King. Each assigned to a mentor, they were guarding His Highness as he visited a colony of dwarves. I was one of two left behind, and it rankled. I worried at the injustice – the indignity – of it all, like a dog worries at a bone. I argued in my head with the Captain, with the King even. So inside my head was I that I didna' hear them coming. Their feet scraped the stones at the last minute, but as I turned something crashed against the side of my head and I knew nummore. When I awoke some hours late, my great, good friends were gone and so were the crown jewels.

I panicked, then, and instead of summoning the guards I ran into the vault to determine what damage had been done. I often wonder what would have happened if I'd followed my training, but I guess it's no use. I didn't. So it was when the next set of guards came to relieve me, they founds the jewels gone, the vault open and me safe, standing in the middle of it.

It was me own da who had to arrest me. It broke him as surely as if I'd put a dagger in his heart. I could see the fire go out of his eyes and his shoulders settle as if the weight of the world had fallen upon them. And mayhap it had. Mayhap it had, at that. Before my trial, he had retired from the disgrace. I never saw him again. I'll not talk about the time I spent in the gaol, and in truth I don't recall much. I believe I was more than half-mad. My first clear memory is of the trial. I had little to say in my defense. After all, I had not seen what happened, not even what they had blindsided me with, and there were a score or more people who testified that they had seen me in town with the thieves, carousing. 'Twas the Captain's testimony that did me in, though. He told them how I'd stood before him, sworn on my own good name. Told him that I took responsibility for them. The judge needed no time to come up with his decision.

'Sir Macauley,' he began. I do not know who it was that cried out, but I will remember the sound until I die. Mayhap it was me." 'Macauley,' the voice said, 'more like Malarkey.' The rest of the crowd took up the chant. "Malarkey, Malarkey," just as they had once called me true name as I ran the lists.

On and on they went until the judge banged his gavel like the crack of a whip. He gave his sentence then, a life of imprisonment, down in the gaol, the only light of day I would see was in the quarry carving blocks out of stone. The judge would not be there later, when they took me from the courtroom to the castle, but the rest of them were. They shouted 'Malarkey' again and again, pelting me with rotten tomatoes, horse droppings, anything foul on which they could place their hands. It was so terrible, so bloody terrible, that the gaol was a relief. That night, I finally gave into despair. I laid on my back, staring at the ceiling, not crying, not thinking. The sun had gone down in my heart. I thought, maybe if I could force myself not to eat long enough, that perhaps I could shorten my sentence a bit. The guards, some of them I'd helped train, brought me a plate of food every night and every night they took it back uneaten.

On the fifth night, I heard the door open and I thought, if I thought anything, that it was just my meal. That is, until I heard my name. My *true* name. It was me old mate Donovan, and he hugged me as if nothing had happened.

'Hurry,' he whispered, pulling a cloak out from under his tabard. 'We have nowt but a few moments.'

I argued with him, told him that I deserved nothing less than this, that he would get in trouble, but he wouldn't hear a word of it.

'You saved me once, mate, and I made a vow. You are guilty of seeing the best in others, of pride, of the follies of youth, but I don't believe you are guilty of more.'

I hugged him once again. "Thanks, Mate," I said, "but for now on I am Malarkey, mayhap it will help me remember. And so I stole out of the city in the dark of night like the thief I was believed to be. I swore that I would never be back." He sighed deeply, staring at the dancing flames. "Looks like another promise I have broken."

Albert was crying, had been since he heard about the trial, and he pulled Malarkey close. He comforted his friend as much as he could, knowing it would never be quite enough.

Chapter Twenty Two

As terrified and despondent as Malarkey was, it was Albert who dallied the next day. He bustled about camp, folding and refolding their supplies.

At nigh on noon, Malarkey came up behind him, placing one flipper on his shoulder. Albert whirled on him. "You don't have to go," he burst out in agony. "Oh Malarkey, you don't have to."

"Do," Jub Jub grumbled. Albert's head whipped around to admonish the bear, but he saw Malarkey nodding. The bird took a deep breath.

"I appreciate you, more than you know, but Jub Jub is right. More than anything else in my life, I have to do this."

Jub Jub flew straight and true, and they reached the great clearing in late afternoon. Jub Jub landed with barely a thump, and both the boy and the bird dismounted. "We all have business here," he said, "I suggest we attend to it."

"We will meet here after the dance? "Albert asked. Malarkey shook his head.

"Maybe, maybe not,' he said. "I ... am not sure where I will be." He caressed Albert's cheek. "Goodbye, lad, if the King wills it, I will see you soon." A look of determination on his face, he strode off towards the castle.

If asked, Albert would have said that Gwytthenia was a vast land, but only sparsely populated. After all, he had covered miles upon seemingly endless miles of the land and, until the Great Forest, had seen only a handful of creatures. If similarly asked, Albert would have expressed, with the manufactured cynicism of one who has been forced to face far too many surprises or obstacles in far too short of a period of time that nothing Gwytthenia had to offer had to power to surprise or overwhelm him. In both cases, he would have been completely and utterly wrong. Thus he stood, his mouth open in wonder and his heartbeat taking on the rhythm of the drums pounding nearby, soaking in more wonder, more awe, than he had seen in the rest of his life combined.

The drums, for example, were not drums in the traditional sense at all. Instead, they came from a group of large, bearded fellows with purple skin and bulbous bellies, sitting cross-legged under some trees. They grinned jovially, slapping their bellies rhythmically with enormous, gnarled hands, and as they opened their mouths the drumbeats reverberated. They were joined by a group of penguins, Macaronis to be exact, and Albert's heart leapt in his throat. He rushed over, checking, but saw almost at once that this group was much younger than Malarkey They still had a bit of down right at the top of their necks, in fact. This cheerful cacophony set the stage for scores of dancers whirling dervish around them. He saw fauns and their larger satyr cousins, tip-toeing nimbly on their dainty hooved feet. He saw more of the beautiful, flowing dryads, swaying as gracefully as the trees themselves, which of course should have been no surprise. He had time to catch glances of a dozen or more creatures that he could not even begin to identify before a young girl with becoming freckles, overlarge eyes, and a cloak made of some sort of grey velvety fur grabbed his hands and whisked him, giggling, into the fray. Albert conveniently forgot, in that moment, that girls terrified him with their sweet-smelling hair and their way of talking in code that those with a Y chromosome cannot possibly understand. Likewise, he forgot that his feet often felt overlarge for the rest of his body and were stubbornly resistant to rhythm. Instead, he just danced, caught in the music, and the merriment, and his partner's laughing eyes. He was passed in the reel, from the sweet becloaked being to a pixie who held daintily to Albert's pointer finger as she swirled in infinity signs and aerial backflips, her feet never touching the ground, to a heavily wrinkled old woman whose back was hunched almost into a U, but who cackled with joy as they spun. Finally, winded and not without a large bit of reluctance, Albert extricated himself, and went in search of refreshments.

  He did not have to look far. He dodged an intriguing game involving large, leather balls, floating hoops, and elaborate hurdles being played by two truly magnificent stags, a beaver, and one of the red, ruffed creatures that he'd seen in the Great Woods. He skirted a veritable plethora of old witches and wizards around a campfire, sharing yarns and blowing moving animals out of their pipe smoke. Suddenly, the feast proper lay in marvelous expansive mouthwateriness in front of him. Bubbling soups, everything from a dark purple conglomeration made of berries to hearty stews, nestled cozily cauldron to platter with sumptuous roasted meats – most of which Albert could not identify – and tarts and cakes and pies enough to satisfy even the most dedicated sweet tooth. Even Tex's enormous repasts seemed like the most meager and unappetizing school lunch next to this, and after weeks of campfire stews, they looked nothing short of heavenly.

Immediately, Albert resolved himself to trying absolutely all of it. After weeks with little food, he hardly felt as though he could do otherwise. *"It would be downright irresponsible,"* he thought with the joy of a grandfather gazing at a Thanksgiving buffet. He wandered from table to table, sampling anything that caught his fancy. A dish of grains, dotted with nuts and berries and spiced heavily, he decided was his favorite, until he tried a cake so light, so airy, that it literally floated inches above the table. He pulled a leg off of a roasted bird, Albert thought it might be fezzant, and with that his favorite dish of all time was replaced again. Most amazingly, none of the plates ever seemed to have less food on them, no matter how many munched upon them, filling themselves by what Albert could only assume was magic. He sampled roasted tubers that tasted of a combination of potato and radish, and a fizzy drink that danced on his tongue and tasted, he would explain later, like flying. Already feeling full but gamely determined to stick to his goal of trying everything, Albert spied skewers of meat that were still on fire, rosy red flames dancing along the meat without burning it, and moved that way.

"Splat!" Without the slightest warning whatsoever, Albert's face was covered with something creamy and sticky-sweet. He could feel it dripping off of his chin onto his already rather road-worn shirt. Incredulously, he cleared the sweet cream out of his eye and looked across the tables. From above a table of meringues shaped like swans, Albert saw two twinkling eyes from immediately below which came a shrill, childish giggle. A large woman, taller than any Albert had ever seen, with thick but pleasant features and square feet strode towards the youngster, her face stern. Albert's heart squeezed in commiseration; he had seen that same look on his own mother's face and was bracing himself for the young giant to be chastised. Apparently, the giantling expected it as well, for it was smiling up in over exaggerated innocence. The mother giant stroked her child's face with one hand, with the other, surreptitiously, she grabbed a large berry tart. Soon, berries covered the youngsters face and most of the ground around her. Albert exploded into shocked laughter, so extreme that his face turned an alarming shade of puce and he bent over, clutching his stomach. Just as he'd started to compose himself, a muffin bounced off of his head. Without even looking for the perpetrator, Albert grabbed some of the whipped tubers that he had sampled earlier and flung them in the general direction from whence the muffin had come. In a matter of moments, it was a free-for all, with bread and muffins, cakes and pies, even legs of roasted meat flying every which way. As the plates continually refilled themselves, either unable to discern eating from fun or equally approving of either, it was as perfect a food fight as anyone can imagine; endless ammo, no clean up required, and certainly no adults coming in roaring with indignation and outrage. Young and old, large and small, humanoid or completely indecipherable the crowd joined in, laughing and cheering. Albert amazed himself by upending a gravy tureen over the head of a gaffer that looked old enough to be his grandfather, and the old man surprised him still more by cackling in glee as the brown drippings rained from his protuberant nose. Such shenanigans were, apparently, not at all uncommon, for those who chose not to join in simply moved dexterously around the edges, dodging flying pies and grabbing a nibble of whatever had caught their fancy, with a bemused smile on their face. After rather a long time, after all, endless food fights may well be every boy's fantasy, Albert decided that he had had enough. He grabbed one last savory, a gloriously browned roll glazed in white and filled with something tart and red that he could not quite identify, and instead of lobbing it, bit into it with relish.

Chapter Twenty Three

Still munching, Albert wandered from the tables to seek out the other joys the feast had to offer. Unsurprisingly, he had completely forgotten his primary goal in this quest. He was not, in fact, there to enjoy the Harvest Ball. He was not there to eat, or even to dance. However, in that moment he was also not a seasoned warrior, not a road-weary adventurer, but in fact just a young boy in the midst of the very epitome of extraordinary. And so he searched, not for a Phim, or the Prince, or a guard, or even the King Himself, but for what seemed to be the next most exciting thing. A crowd of raucous cheering seemed to have promise, and so he followed his ears in that direction. Soon, he found himself at the back of a wall of people. They crowded around, a veritable throng, elbowing and jostling to gain a better view. Small, green-skinned men with long, pointy ears and positively saber-like noses circulated. "Place your bets," they buzzed. "Place your bets, here." Spectators would then wave their hands in the air and in exchange for their twigs the goblin would laboriously make some marks on a small piece of parchment, licking the graphite each time with a tongue as blue as a blueberry. Albert wound his way through the mass, trying not to bump up against anyone and failing miserably.

At one point, careening off a large grey creature who reeked of mead, he bumped into one of the goblins. "A bet, lad?" the goblin asked, looking him up and down with shrewd eyes. "Muskin has the best returns, guaranteed." Albert stepped back, his palms held up. "No ... no, I ... I don't ..." he stammered.

"Off with ye, then," the goblin replied, and turned back to the marks who eagerly waved their coin. Abruptly, Albert burst forth from the crowd and face to fur with an enormous roan flank. His eyes wider than his mouth, Albert followed the flank up and up, over and over until eventually the fur turned to deeply tanned and sharply chiseled flesh and finally to a fiercely bearded face.

"Here for the race?" the centaur grumbled, not unkindly.

"I think so?" Albert asked.

"Brave colt," the centaur chuckled.

"Foolish cub," another voice replied, and to Albert's astonishment a Plainsmen approached. The Plainsmen had the trunk of a man. Its arms and legs were covered in fur that was not tawny like Ahoka's, but the spotted fur of a cheetah. Even the face was vaguely feline, the eyes a brilliant emerald green with slitted pupils, and long whiskers sprouted from a split upper lip. From its back, giant wings sprouted, standing taller than the being itself. They, too, were different from Ahoka's both in size and in color. Albert thought about asking if they were from a different tribe, but thought that might be offensive. After all, his hair was "no color brown" while his mother's was deep chocolate. The Plainsman continued. "In my tribe, warriors train for years for the honor to compete, and many have died in the attempt. Once, one of our own won the whole competition, only to have his heart burst at the finish line as the crowd cheered."

"That's true," the centaur grumbled, "I'll never forget Moonbow, crushed under the feet of his brother in the final heat."

Albert ran his hands through his hair, and the bracelet on his wrist caught the attention of the Plainsman.

"Where did you get that?" he asked, motioning at the beads.

"I... a friend gave it to me," he said. "I helped her out once, in the prarie."

The Plainsman almost smiled. "You must have been a great help, indeed. A friendship bracelet is no small honor. Honor your friend, then. Step aside. This is no place for you."

"Don't pay any attention to them," said a low voice at Albert's shoulder. "I think you're very brave to try." Albert snapped his head to the side and instantly regretted it. Having spent all of his life with two eyes, he would have been rather dismayed to suddenly find himself with one and yet, encountering a very long and very sharp horn just millimeters from his pupil, he very nearly found himself making some difficult adjustments. As it was, disaster was averted, and upon following the horn to its owner, Albert found himself gazing on what was possibly the most beautiful creature Albert had ever seen. It is safe to say that many, if not most, people spend a great deal of life hoping in their secret hopes that someday they will encounter a unicorn, that they are not mythological, that somewhere in some hidden part of the world, they exist. Still, Albert was not prepared for what meeting a unicorn would actually mean. If asked, he would have said that they were a brilliant white horse, with a horn, and be hard pressed to give any details save that. What stood in front of Albert was the sleekest, most muscular equine creature he had ever seen, his coat not white, but glistening black. Not glistening as though the coat reflected the light around it, but actually, truly glistening. Upon closer inspection, Albert noticed that the points of light were not random, but were in fact Gwytthenian constellations and he smiled as he saw the turtle Tukka, as though greeting an old friend. The tail on the unicorn was not the tail of a horse. In fact, most unicorns would be flabbergasted and perhaps a bit offended to discover that that is how they are depicted here in what we foolishly believe is the real world. It resembled nothing more than the tail of a lion, albeit a midnight lion, long and sinewy and ending in a tuft. The horn with which Albert had nearly had an unfortunate interaction started out black as well before fading in a glorious ombre to a silver that matched the stars exactly.

"Thank you," Albert said, mystified, "but I'm not actually competing. I'm just here to watch."

"Oh good," the unicorn whinnied. "You did seem a bit small, though I didn't want to say it. My name is Nidan."

"Albert," the boy replied. "So you are racing, then?"

"Oh yes. My parents didn't want me to, of course. They are frightened that I will get hurt, or worse, that I will dishonor the herd. My mother tore at the turf for days when I told her. But I've been training with my friends every day, hours and hours, training until my hooves bled. I'm going to win!"

Albert grinned. He liked Nidan, plucky and determined, and he hoped with all of his heart that the unicorn would, in fact, win. He did feel a prickle of fear as well, not entirely sure what dishonor on the herd would mean, or what the consequences of such would be.

"I hope you do!" he said, raising his hand to pat the horse on his neck and then thinking better of it, trying to disguise the motion by scratching his neck instead.

"Will you bet on me?" Nidan asked. "Nobody will bet on me, not against the likes of them." He tossed his enormous head at the other competitors in the ring.

"I don't have any twigs," Albert said, regretfully, "but I'll be cheering for you!"

"Good!" Nidan whinnied. Suddenly, the great blast of a horn split the air and the energy in the crowd changed, electrified. "I have to go," Nidan said, and Albert saw his eyes narrow, his muscles tense.

Albert stepped back deliberately, lest someone more official make the same mistake that the centaur had, and he found himself in significantly over his head. Carefully, he wedged himself in a small space amongst the spectators. Nidan, the centaur, the Plainsman, and at least a score of others lined up behind a deep furrow that had been scratched in the turf. Craning his neck, Albert could see a long stretch of flat, cleared ground and at the end two tiny winged figures who were shooting fountains of colored sparks into the air.

"Last call for bets!" the goblins called, and Albert found himself clenching and unclenching his hands in anticipation. The horn sounded again, and the racers were off in a cloud of dust and flying sod. Albert could not hear the footsteps over the roaring of the crowd, but he could feel them, vibrating the ground until it became difficult to stand.

"Go Nidan!" he screamed. "Go!" He yelled so loud that his throat felt scratchy and raw, yet the enthusiasm of the crowd drowned out his words. Still, he could not stop, hoping somehow the unicorn would hear him, would know that someone believed in him. Suddenly, the spectators gasped in unison and Albert saw, in the distance, flying dirt and flailing hooves. He clutched at his mouth until he saw the cocky but kind centaur from earlier rise to his feet, brushing the dirt from his pelt. Several creatures moaned their dismay; he had been highly placed in the ranks and veritable forests of twigs had exchanged hopes in the belief that he would win. The centaur plodded off the racetrack, his shoulders slumped. Still, the race went on. Seconds later, it was over. Albert could not see who had won, but word moved nearly as quickly up the row as the racers had moved down.

"The unicorn!"

"T'was the twilight unicorn."

"Are you sure?"

"I'da never believed it of him." Several spectators, poor sports all, groaned loudly, still, more cheered in adoration, Albert included.
He rushed forward with the rest of offer congratulations.

"Did you see me? I was the fastest!" the unicorn said again and again. "Now the King will notice me for sure!" Albert found himself at the front of the pack.

"You're here to see the King, too?" Albert asked.

Nidan nodded. "I want to be a part of His guard. I'm no penguin, I know, but I'm fast! The fastest!" He whinnied in joy, his hooves pawing at the air.

Albert liked the idea of seeing the King accompanied by the hero of the day. He liked that quite a lot. It seemed much better than wandering in by himself. "Maybe we could-"

"It's you!" a high-pitched voice cut through the air. Albert thought nothing of it until a tiny hand clutched at his hair, pulling him close. "It's you, it's you, it's you! At least, I think it's you. You looked different then." The creature pulled out a wand just slightly larger than a toothpick and siphoned off some of the mud and whipped cream from Albert's face. "Oh it is!" she squealed in delight, her pink skin growing even rosier and her iridescent wings pounding madly at the air.

"Yes," Albert replied when he could get a word in edgewise. "It's me ... but who are you?!"

The fairy clapped her wings against her cheeks, her rosebud mouth falling open.

"You don't remember me?" she exclaimed. "But then, you wouldn't. When we met, you were asleep." She giggled like the chiming of bells. "I'm the one who brought you here, me and-" she flashed magenta. "Dewdron! We have to find him." She grasped the tip of Albert's ear with a hand that was surprisingly, painfully strong and started dragging him through the crowd. Albert had to run to keep up, his toes barely touching the ground. She finally came to a stop in front of a small group intently playing a game that consisted of stones and sticks.

"Dewdron!" the fairy squealed. "Look!" One of the small wrinkled creatures turned, his brown eyes growing larger as he looked Albert up and down. The Leafybe gasped and leapt to his feet. He barely came up to Albert's thighs and his clothes hung on him, as wrinkled and brown as he face.

"We need to tell everyone," he said. "It's a glorious day." And they were on the run again.

"Wait!" Albert called to no avail. "I don't even know why I'm here, or who you are!"

Moonlor squealed again. "You will!"

Soon, they found themselves on a large dais in the center of the clearing. Albert had trouble climbing up, and so the fairy on one side and the brownie on the other grabbed him by the shoulders and lifted him up. Albert yelped in amazement at their strength.

"Stay there. Look impressive. I'm going to announce you," Moonlor ordered.

"Wait, announce me to wh-" but she had already turned away and was yelling into the crowd."

Attention!" Moonlor bellowed. It was a very high-pitched bellow. Still, Albert could barely hear on over the jolly cacophony that surrounded them.

"Attention!" she yelled again, higher but not necessarily louder. She got the same result. Frustrated, the fairy stomped her foot and pulled a tiny dropper out of her bag. She dribbled a bit down her throat, and Albert watched in amazement, and not a little bit of digust as her neck swelled and bulged. She looked like a rainbow bullfrog. "ATTENTION! " This time her voice thundered as though from the heavens, themselves with such power that the branches of the trees parted outward and more than a few of the dancers tumbled over. The noise of the feast stopped like a switch had been flipped, and soon Albert felt the pressure of hundreds of eyes on him. Moonlor took several deep breaths and Albert broke out into a sweat. His chest felt tight. He scanned the crowd, nearly panicked.

"I'd rather fight the spiders than be here now," he thought to himself. At least with the spiders he knew what

to do. Suddenly, he saw Jub Jub's brown, loving eyes resting on him, a friendly smile visible through the remnants of something sweet and sticky still on his face. Albert took a deep breath and grinned back. Whatever lay ahead, he thought, it can't be worse than what I've already faced.

"Go on," he said to Moonlor, "I'm ready."

"As you know," Moonlor began, "Gwytthenia has faced dark times as of late. So dark, so mysterious, that the King thought we should get help to find the source. Members of all races, from all corners of the world have been affected. And so He in His wisdom, located our champion." The crowd cheered. "He found a warrior, someone who has shown himself to be brave, true, and selfless."

Albert's chest felt tight again, this time with pride. *I am a hero,* he thought wonderingly. He never would have imagined, not in a million years, that he would be a hero, but was surprised to discover that after everything he had been through, he actually felt like one. More than that, he discovered to his delight that he wanted to be one. A grin split Albert's face, and he began to strut, just a bit, across the stage, following the fairy as she flitted back and forth.

"Someone smart enough to solve this mystery and strong enough to face whatever it might be."

The cheering grew louder and Albert's heart felt as though it might explode. Finally, *finally*, he was special.

Finally, he was enough. He thought of all of the times he walked out on the baseball diamond for the first time when he congratulated the other team. The times he worked on homework until his eyes were grainy, only to get, at best, a B. The times his mother pushed him aside. Moonlor continued.

"We brought him here, Dewdron and I. We found him and got him through the portal. But then," she swallowed and paled a little bit, "we lost him in a storm. I thought," her voice trembled. "I thought that all hope was lost. The King told me, though, He told me not to give up. To let my heart be light. He knew the plans He had, plans that could not be cast aside by wind and rain. And He was right! I present to you our champion, our hero! Citizens of Gwytthenia, I present SAMUEL CHRISTOPHER MCCUBBINS!"

The roar of the crowd was overwhelmed by the ringing in Albert's own head. Suddenly, cold, shivering, he choked back a sob and ran from the stage.

Chapter Twenty Four

Albert Robert Thomas Jackson was a heartbroken boy. He had fallen from the blackened skies of a thunderstorm and trekked countless miles under a burning sun. He had defeated the Chordra, soared through the air on the back of a winged bear, and battled a legion of bloodthirsty, carnivorous spiders; but even after all of that, he was no one special. After all of that, he was still just absolutely normal. Albert had slipped away in the chaos that ensued following Moonlor's pronouncement, and now entertained only the company of himself, far from the confused murmurs of the partygoers. He was sore. After fleeing, he had tried valiantly to get inside the castle. He had circled the outer wall and flung himself one at a time against each of the twelve gates. Albert's shoulders ached and he had a large scratch down one of them, one that he picked at as mercilessly as he did his own misery. He had screamed, demanded entry until he was hoarse, and still the gates had not opened, not one.

Now, he sat on the crumbling stone wall of an old reflecting pool. Moss hung thick from the great trees, and delicate white night flowers sent their perfume into the air. The full moon shone down on the surface of the water, turning it into a looking glass. Albert stared down at his reflection. The face that looked back at him still did not look like a hero, though it was much changed from that of the boy that Moonlor and Dewdron had peered upon those weeks before. He was no longer plump; the journey had done that much for him. The sun had browned his skin and brought out more freckles, and his hair was shaggier than ever. Yes, he was leaner, tanner, and more rugged perhaps, but still his face was not one that would inspire the troops to charge into battle, that would bring an end to evil that would be sought out of everyone else and he had been foolish to believe it was so. Albert started to cry, the tears dripping off the tip of his nose and causing ripples on the surface of the water that moved out and out from the center. His head hurt. It pounded, but more than that it reverberated with unheard voices.

"I just don't want you near me right now," his mother said. "Three cheers for Samuel," shouted the Gwytthenians. On and on they went, his own more than any: "You're not special, you're nothing. You're nobody. If your father were alive, he'd be ashamed. He wouldn't want you, either. Nobody wants you, Albert. Nobody wants you." Suddenly he heard another voice. It was deep, dark, sibilant.

"Ahhh, that's where you're wrong, dear boy," it said. "*I* want you." Albert startled. He looked behind him, into the woods, but there was no one there. The branches above his head were empty as well. He heard the voice again. "Down here, my son," the voice hissed.
"Look down here."

Albert looked down by his feet. The water in the pool was rippling, and his reflection was gone. The liquid had turned murky brown and from it, two fierce golden eyes glared. "I've been watching you, boy, for quite a long time, and I think you're very special. Very sssssspecial indeed." As the voice continued, the water began to steam.

Albert's voice quavered. "Wh…who are you?" he asked.

"I am something very special indeed. I am no King, bound by rules and laws and locked away in a castle like a coward. I am free to go where I want, to do what I please. I answer to no one. I see into the hearts of men; I know their dreams and fears just as I know yours. I have tasted freedom…and power…and courage. .. and I know something extra-ordinary when I see it. You, my son, are extraordinary. Or could be. Come with me, boy. *I* want you. Come with me. Be with me and I will give you everything. I will take the pain away. Then, we will see how special you can be."

"I'm not…" Albert started. "I don't…" he began again. "Malarkey s…said the King would fix it. He said that He'd make everything all right."

"Send you back home, you mean," the voice replied. "Send you back to a mother who can't even look at you, to teachers who can hardly remember your name? Is that what you want? What sign has the king even given that he wants you anyway? Maybe they're wrong, the penguin and the bear and the fairy. After all, has the king reached out to you? I found you easily, but then again I wanted to." The voice laughed, and for a moment Albert saw the white flash of a tooth in the water. The boy sat, quite for a long time, chewing on the ragged skin to the side of his left thumbnail, and watching the steam as it roiled and eddied on the warm summer air.

Finally, he sighed. "What do I do?" he asked.

The eyes flashed, brilliant and metallic. "It's easy," the voice growled. "Easy as sliding into the tub, easy as jumping in a lake on a hot summer day. Step into the water. Hurry boy, the time has come. You can walk away and be nothing, or, or you can come with me, and know what it is to be a very…special…boy."

Slowly, slowly as if in a dream, Albert came to his feet. He brushed the grit and moss off the back of his legs without taking his eyes off the water. He clenched his jaw and unclenched it, the muscles bulging in his cheeks. He clasped his hands into fists. He took a great deep breath and stepped off the wall… onto the ground behind him. He took one step backwards, then two, and finally he turned around. The creature howled with fury, and from the path into the clearing a new voice spoke, soft and still.

"It was well done, lad. That way never leads to anywhere but heartache and death."

Albert startled and whirled around to face a man standing at the edge of the shadows. The man was tall and lean. He wore a crown and a purple tunic and though he smiled warmly, a fine network of lines wreathed dark eyes that were somehow sad.

"You saw that too? You heard that?" The man nodded. "Well if it's so bad," Albert said, "why didn't you stop me?"

The man shrugged and smiled. "It wasn't my decision to make," he said gently.

Albert took this in, considered it, and looked for a long time at the figure standing before him. He crossed his arms across his chest and tilted his head cheekily. "I suppose you're the King," he said.

"No," the man replied, "but I will take you to Him. I am the Prince, and my Father sent me for you. He'd like to see you in His chambers."

Albert snickered meanly. "No, no He doesn't. I tried to get in, but He wouldn't let me." The Prince stepped forward and laid His hand gently on Albert's head. Albert felt the muscles in his neck and shoulders, muscles that had been tense and drawn for so long that he no longer noticed, suddenly relax, and he almost wept with the relief.
The anger flowed out of him, he could almost feel it pouring away.

"Ah, but you can only get to Him through me. I am the way." He leaned forward. "May I?"

At first, Albert didn't know what He was talking about, but then he had a flash of His mother. Not too long before, Albert had decided that he no longer wanted to be kissed on the lips, not even on the cheek. However, he would deign to allow her, every now and then, to kiss his forehead. Just before she did, she would stand just as the

Prince was standing now. Albert closed his eyes and nodded. The Prince gently pressed his lips against the boy's sweaty brow. Albert felt the warmth from that kiss, felt it pass through him, and without thinking he threw his arms around the noble one.

"Oh it hurts," he wailed, sobbing. "It hurts so badly. I've been so scared for so long." The Prince hugged him close.

"I know," He said

Albert cried loudly, gustily, like a very small child. He cried for his father; he cried for his mother; he cried for the carousel horse that he could not save. Most of all, though, he cried for himself and for the hope that he felt was lost. The Prince held him until the storm had passed, and then stepped back, discreetly admiring the patterns of the leaves while the boy hiccupped and wiped his face.

Once Albert had collected himself, the Prince held out his hand. "Are you ready?" he asked.

Albert scuffed at the moss at his feet. "Do I have to go?"

The Prince shook his head, "No. Just as before, it is your decision and yours alone. No one can make you. But Albert," the Prince kneeled down so that His eyes were level with Albert's. He reached out and squeezed the boy's shoulder gently. Immediately, Albert's shoulder grew very warm, and his heart slowed until it no longer felt too big and too heavy for his chest. "We hope that you will come."

The Prince stood and walked slowly to the foot of the path that lead from the garden. There, he paused and turned back to face the boy. Albert wavered. He wanted to go. He wanted to walk beside the Prince, to listen to His voice and feel the comfort of His hand on his shoulder once again. To pretend that He was with his father. He wanted to go and he knew it was good and right. Still, though, his feet felt rooted to the ground and the farther away the Prince moved the more the fear grew. The voices, those that had all but disappeared, started to hammer at his brain once again.

"Nobody wants you, nobody wants you, you are not the one."

Albert felt a bubble rise in his chest. He gritted his teeth, but still it found its way out. "You don't understand!" Albert cried. "He'll send me home. It was all a mistake and He'll send me home and I... I don't want to go!" He was panting, stomping with rage and fear.

Once Albert's breathing had returned to normal, the Prince spoke once again. "It's a funny thing, mistakes. Men make them, and beasts. Even penguins. Fairies make them; dwarves too. I have never, though, known my Father to make one. But Albert," and here He reached His hand out towards the boy, "if you don't go to Him, you will never know."

Albert nodded, slowly, and sniffed loudly. He took the hand that was offered to him and walked in silence with the Prince, out of the garden with the fountain. They walked slowly, the pair, and the Prince shortened His strides so that He stayed by Albert's side. They held hands as they walked, and while Albert would have normally thought that this was odd, this time he took comfort from the warmth. It was as though, for a brief moment, he was a young child walking with his Dad. They passed under trees hung heavy with moss, just to the side of a stone wall that appeared to be even more ancient than the fountain. In the distance, Albert could hear the joyful tootling of a flute and feel in his chest the deep bass of the drums. The Ball had started once again. After a few moments, Albert and the Prince came to one of the gates that Albert had not tried before. Royal Penguins, in full battle gear and splendid uniforms, now graced each side. They stood at full attention, their beady eyes fixed on a point on what would be the horizon if the trees did not block the way, and as Albert and the Prince drew near they raised their swords in salute. The Prince laid His hand on the door and it slowly swung open on its iron hinges.

Chapter Twenty Five

Albert followed the Prince through hallways made of stone. It was like no stone Albert had ever seen, seamless, flawless. He ran his hands along the walls and they felt like glass. They the pair turned one last corner, Albert almost bumped into Malarkey, who was rushing out, tears falling from his eyes. " Malarkey," Albert yelled. The bird turned, looking at Albert with elation. "What happened?"

"Redemption, lad,' Malarkey exclaimed, "There may be redemption after all." He pulled Albert into a fierce hug. "You'd better not keep him waiting, boy," he said, and then was gone through a door that slammed shut behind him.

Albert's mouth was suddenly dry. He swallowed twice, his tongue clicking in the back of his throat. He glanced around, searching for anyone who could go with him, anyone who could, if necessary, push him through the doors. There was no one. He squeezed his eyes, wishing desperately that when he opened them he would be at home, back in the mountains, anywhere where he would not have to make this decision. He remembered what his father told him once, in the days before he got sick, talking about war and how he had the courage to move ahead. "Sometimes not making a decision *is* a decision." 'I could do that,' Albert thought to himself. *"I could just ... not decide,"* but his stomach flipped and flopped at the thought, and he knew what he had to do. On legs that felt like they belonged to someone else, he took one step forward, and then another. He put his hand on the door and pushed. He expected it to be heavy, reluctant to move on the huge iron hinges, but he found it swung easily. Albert stepped inside.

The throne room was smaller than he expected, cozy. Torches hung on sconces every few feet, with beautiful tapestries between them. The floor was covered in throw rugs that felt amazing on Albert's road-weary feet. A huge fireplace dominated the far end, crackling merrily, and a pot simmering above sent the aroma of exotic spices wafting through the room. The throne faced the fire. It looked unlike any throne that Albert had imagined. It wasn't golden, or silver, or even bronze. In fact, it looked like nothing more than a giant armchair, albeit one with beautiful wooden carvings. "Mercy" was written across the top, surrounded by vines. Woven into the tapestries, carved into the wood, Albert saw the creatures of Gwytthenia. He saw dryads and fauns, unicorns and penguins. Pixies and Leafybes peered out from behind flowers. So enraptured was he, that it wasn't until Albert heard the quiet clearing of a throat that he remembered Who he was there to see. His jaw clenched in determination, he walked forward. Once he got to the end of the throne room he turned towards the figure and kneeled, breathing heavily. The King laid his hand gently on Albert's shoulder.

"My boy," He said. "My dear boy, you've come to me at last."

Albert stared at the floor, following the curls and turns of the weaving.

"Your Majesty, I-"

"-Are surely in need of some refreshment," the King interrupted. "If you would, son, please ladle us some cider from the pot. It will fuel our conversation nicely, I believe."

Trembling, Albert lifted his head. Merry blue eyes twinkled at him from a face cobwebbed with wrinkles. The bottom half of the king's face was nearly obscured by a long, white beard, but Albert could see his mouth, smiling gently. The King's shoulders were broad, strong, though drooping slightly as if bearing a huge weight. His right hand bore a golden ring with a ruby as large as a robin's egg.

"But I-"

"-Get us some cider, son," the King said, gently but firmly. "By the time I've finished my tale, your questions may be answered

Frustrated, Albert did as he was told. He raised the goblet to his lips, breathing in the heady mix of apples, cinnamon, and more than a few spices he could not name.

"Tell me," the King said. "How do you like my Kingdom?"

Albert stared for a long moment, looking at the swirls in the steam from his cider, before he answered. "When I first came here, I didn't like it a all," he admitted. "The mountains were freezing and Malarkey, he was very mean back then." He paused. "Well, I guess he wasn't mean, really, just scared, but he wasn't the most friendly. Then the swamps." He shuddered. "I did not like the swamps at all. That Chordra, he was awful. For the first couple of weeks after we left Malarkey's hut, I cried myself to sleep almost every night. I wanted to go home."

"And then? "the King prompted.

"And then, I don't know, I found out that there are some parts of your Kingdom that are really beautiful. Difficult. Harsh, you know? But beautiful. And, and the creatures I met here, they're the best friends I've ever had." The King nodded.

"There are many wonderful creatures here," he concurred. "Good ... and bad, just like most of life. Of course, the bad has been spreading recently. There's an evil in my land. Great evil. It's growing daily. If it isn't stopped soon, all of Gwytthenia will ..." He stopped.
Albert noticed his eyes were wet.

"Die?" Albert volunteered. The King sighed.

"Worse."

Albert's eyes widened. "Worse? What's worse than death?"

"A great many things, son," the King replied. "This evil, it destroys from the inside out. It takes everything that is good and true and twists it, turns it dark. If allowed to continue all things here will be like the Chordra, or worse. I need you. I need someone who can find the source of the evil and eliminate it."

"Eliminate? You mean kill?"

The king looked down. "Cure if you can. Always cure first if you can. But, if not, then yes."

"But why do you need someone else to do it? You have to know what it is, even if you don't you could just ride out, find out where it was, you could eliminate it instantly." Tears coursed slowly down the King's cheeks.

"I could, indeed, and once upon a time I would have. Once I roamed about my Kingdom at will, dealing aid and justice as the needs required. Once there wasn't a citizen of my Kingdom who could say they had never been greeted by the King. But now ... the members of my Kingdom ... they don't want me to. They've put me in a box, sealed me in my castle. They want the King that they imagine. A genie. One who can and will make everything better with the wave of His hand. They don't want to believe that I grow sad, or weary, or angry. Especially not angry. And so I cannot do what must be done. But you ... you are a hero that they can accept, and love. That's why I called you."

Suddenly, Albert was shaking, his fists and his teeth grinding together. He felt tears, hot ones, rising to his eyes and making his nose feel stuffy. He held his breath with the effort of holding in the words that wanted to come.

"Why are you so angry, son?" the King asked gently.

"Because it isn't me ou want!" Albert screamed, red-faced. "I fought the Chordra. I...I made it through the mountains and destroyed giant spiders. I love Gwytthenia!. I love *You* and still You never wanted me! Just like my mom...just like everyone." Albert felt a weathered hand rest gently on his hanging head.

"Who said I didn't want you?" the King asked.

"Everyone!" Albert exclaimed. "Moonlor, Malarkey, the whole cheering crowd told me. They told me when they cheered for his name. Samuel's. They think I'm Samuel. They think I am my perfect, handsome, talented cousin. If they knew, if you knew me, you wouldn't want me

"But I do know you, Albert Robert Thomas Jackson. I've seen you, you know. I saw you in your land, crying for the death of your father, the despair of your mother. I saw you as you never gave up hope, never stopped trying. And I saw you here. Every hardship you faced, every joy you shared, I was there. And it just confirmed that it was you that I wanted all along."

"You knew?" Albert admonished. "You knew I was here? Why didn't you rescue me? Why did you let me go through all of that? I almost died!"

The King gazed at the flames, the golden light dancing over his face. "If I had, if I had appeared before you in the mountains, stood there and told you who I was... who you are... would you have believed me?"

Albert opened his mouth, closed it, and opened it again. "No," he said at last.

"No," the King agreed. "It was only after everything you'd seen and everything you'd done that you could have believed me. You had to come to Me, no matter the stakes. And, you helped one of my own find his way back to me."

"The storm? You did that?"

The King frowned, his eyes dipped downward. "Did it? No, lad. I do not make evil for those I love. But I knew what would be, and I knew I could use it. That I did. Do you hate me for it?"

Albert was aghast. "I wish you could have found an easier way."

"Oh, me too, son. Me too. But I must work for the good of all for all of time and that, precisely, is the kind of situation that the people I rule cannot understand. That sometimes you have to hurt to heal. But I believed that one of the things that was special about YOU, about *you*, Albert, was that you could. Can you?"

Albert thought of his dad and his fourth time through rehab. Fifth? He and his mother visited him in the midst of it all, and his father's sweaty body, the vein pulsing in his forehead, the panicked look in his eyes, were seared into Albert's memory. "I can't do it," his father had sobbed, "it hurts." Albert also remembered, however, what he had said. "Only for a little while, Dad. It will hurt, but then you'll be better." He remembered also how heartbroken he had felt when his dad had failed. And failed. And failed one last fatal time.

"Yes," he murmured, "I can understand."

"Will you do it? Will you find the evil that plagues us and drive it out?" the King asked. Albert stared at the tapestry on the wall next to him. He wondered if Jardine had woven it. Finally, he nodded.

"I will," he said at last, "but… but I don't feel like I can do it alone." The King smiled and nodded to the Prince who walked to the door. Albert hadn't even noticed Him come in.

"I don't think you'll have to."

The doors creaked open, and Albert saw, waiting behind them, the smiling faces of Malarkey and Jub Jub.

"You did it, lad!" Malarkey squawked, rushing into the throne room. Albert caught him in a hug with one hand, and Jub Jub with another. He saw, then, the others: Moonlor and Dewdron, the unicorn, they all followed Malarkey and Jub Jub in.

"You'll go with me?" he asked.

Dewdron nodded. Moonlor glimmered.

"I hoped the King would notice me, and He did!" the unicorn exclaimed.

"Jub Jub go." The bear beast rumbled.

"Shut the doors," the King commanded. "Your journey is just beginning."

Acknowledgements

It is common practice among authors, this author to be precise, to thank in the acknowledgements those without whom the book would not have come to be. Generally, we are speaking symbolically and perhaps a bit hyperbolically, or what we mean is that this book would not have come about in this precise fashion. However, in this case there are three without whom this book would literally not exist in any fashion, and I'd like to acknowledge them first.

To Kathy- AT one point you held the only draft of this novel. The rest of them had been lost or destroyed and with them any hopes I had of completing this. I didn't even know you had it until you pulled it out of your filing cabinet. Without that copy, this whole project would have been lost. Thank you so much, and I love you.

To my graphic designer turned best friend turned husband – You then took that one lonely hard copy draft and painstakingly retyped it, not only encouraging me to start again, but also ensuring that it would never be lost. That was just one of the many sacrifices that you've made for me, this story, and our family. You are one of my greatest blessings.

And to God – You have me this life, this idea, and this talent. I believe that a large part of the reasoning for that was so that, maybe, I could teach others about the God I know and who loves me. A God who is loving, merciful, and just, who knows that we are each unique and precious images of Him, none of whom are truly Absolutely Normal.

They say that it takes a village to raise a child, but it takes a village of a different sort to raise a book. I would be remiss if I did not take a moment to thank the following members of my village.

To Douglas Gresham – Your gentle but honest critiques elevated this novel immensely. You caused me to grow as a writer and I cannot thank you enough. It was an honor speaking with you.

To Vikki Becker, my editor and friend – thank you for helping make this book the best version of itself, and also providing a safe haven for my family.

To the Beta readers: Martha, Sarah, DeAnna, and Alma – Between the four of you, you caught loopholes, inconsistences, and provided me with encouragement and insight. Thank you for the gifts of time and love.

To Martha, again – Thank you for the song, the compass, and the map. Thank you for saving me when I needed saving.

To my adopted sister Sh – you inspire me every day to move forward fearlessly in my faith. Your friendship is an amazing gift.

To my Dad – thank you for the magic pens and for dutifully buying each of my books even though you don't like to read.

To my Mom – Thank you for believing that this day would come. I promise to finish Harmony Shaw someday.

Finally, to my children- Thank you for cheering me on and giving up your time to be with me on every step of this adventure. Thank you for making me a better person and showing me the wonder of every day.

Also by Line By Lion

Also by Line By Lion

Also by Line By Lion

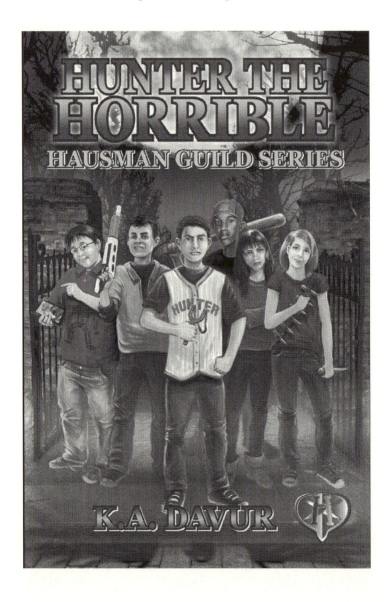

Also by Line By Lion

A Touch of Frost

What is happening to Yasmine?

A novel by
S Hafreth

Made in the USA
Middletown, DE
13 January 2022